"None of us like to have our privacy invaded," Janna said defensively.

"I'm sure you don't yourself, Mr. Santine."

"You're right. I hate it," Rafe admitted. "But then I've reached a position where I don't have to stand for it anymore, while you're still vulnerable. Very vulnerable." He suddenly reached out and touched the curve of her cheek. "You have incredibly beautiful bones."

"My grandmother is a full-blooded Cherokee Indian," Janna said quietly, forcing herself to sit still under that curiously gentle touch. It was almost completely impersonal, so why did she feel as if her skin was burning beneath his fingers?

"Interesting," Rafe said softly, as his hand dropped away from her face and he slowly leaned back in hs chair. "Then your aversion to captivity is probably inherited, which would only make it stronger. I'm making progress."

"Progress?" Janna asked warily, her brown eyes fixed on his with the look of a gazelle that suddenly senses danger.

"You're something of a challenge, Janna," Rafe drawled. "I can't remember ever being so intrigued with a woman before. I suppose it's that skittish, wild aura about you that arouses all my aggressive hunting instincts . . ."

WHAT ARE *LOVESWEPT* ROMANCES?

They are stories of true romance and touching emotion. We believe those two very important ingredients are constants in our highly sensual and very believable stories in the *LOVESWEPT* line. Our goal is to give you, the reader, stories of consistently high quality that may sometimes make you laugh, sometimes make you cry, but are always fresh and creative and contain many delightful surprises within their pages.

Most romance fans read an enormous number of books. Those they truly love, they keep. Others may be traded with friends and soon forgotten. We hope that each *LOVESWEPT* romance will be a treasure—a "keeper." We will always try to publish

LOVE STORIES YOU'LL NEVER FORGET
BY AUTHORS YOU'LL ALWAYS REMEMBER

The Editors

LOVESWEPT • 32

Iris Johansen

The Lady and the Unicorn

BANTAM BOOKS • TORONTO • NEW YORK • LONDON • SYDNEY

THE LADY AND THE UNICORN

A Bantam Book / January 1984

*LOVESWEPT and the wave device are trademarks of
Bantam Books, Inc.*

ISBN 0-553-21626-0

Published simultaneously in the United States and Canada

*Bantam Books are published by Bantam Books, Inc. Its trade-
mark, consisting of the words "Bantam Books" and the por-
trayal of a rooster, is Registered in U.S. Patent and Trademark
Office and in other countries. Marca Registrada. Bantam
Books, Inc., 666 Fifth Avenue, New York, New York 10103.*

PRINTED IN THE UNITED STATES OF AMERICA

O   0 9 8 7 6 5 4 3 2 1

One

Janna breathed a profound sigh of relief as she settled herself in the rented blue Chevette and backed out of the motel parking lot. The last hour had been more of a strain than she'd anticipated, and she was relieved that she no longer had to pretend a confidence she was far from feeling. Another fifteen minutes with David, and her guilt and apprehension about tonight might have tempted her to tell him the truth, and that would have been totally foolish. If the professor knew of her plans for tonight, he would never let her make the attempt no matter how desperate they felt about the fate of their cause.

She'd received explicit instructions from the rental-car clerk at the airport as to how to get to Santine's Castle, which was becoming something of a local Carmel landmark, and had no trouble following the directions to the fabulous seaside mansion. She almost wished she *had* experienced difficulties that would have kept her from thinking on her way to her destination. Once she'd made up her mind, she'd thought there would be no second thoughts to plague her, but she found this was not the case.

Damn it, why hadn't the man consented to see her? Then this little adventure tonight wouldn't have been necessary. She'd tried desperately to convince the secretary in Santine's San Francisco office how important it was that she at least have the opportunity to lay her request before the woman's employer, but had been told that Santine was recuperating from a serious illness at his home in Carmel and couldn't be disturbed. The wall of resistance from his employees was as hard and cold as Santine himself.

Well, perhaps that wasn't quite accurate, she thought wryly. According to the gossip columns, Santine was far from cold. He reportedly changed mistresses as often as he changed shirts, and seemed to have no problem in keeping them very contented for the brief periods that he maintained them. But there was no doubt at all about his hardness. His reputation for ruthless brilliance had been earned over years of fighting to the top of the economic ladder from the slums of New York. From what she'd read about him, Janna knew that Santine had started as a construction worker at sixteen, and by the time he was twenty-three he had owned the company. From there he'd risen like a runaway comet, branching out into real estate, computers, and oil. The list was staggering, and everything he touched turned to pure gold. Now, at thirty-eight, he was practically a legend, a self-made billionaire wielding more power than many heads of state. Unfortunately, his emergence at the top of the mountain hadn't seemed to mellow him. His takeovers of smaller companies occurred with sharklike regularity even now that he was an economic giant.

And this was the man she was going to force her way in to see tonight? For a moment Janna doubted her own sanity. Then her chin lifted with determination and her lips quickly tightened with resolution. No, she was not going to let Santine's reputation intimidate her. Once she was actually in his presence, surely she could find a way of appealing to his softer side. The man couldn't be granite all the way through, despite the stories about him. She really had no choice now that she'd tried every other means at her command to earn a reprieve for the wildlife reserve. There was no way that she was going to let their landlord's greed send those animals back into captivity.

She rounded the curve, and caught her breath as she saw her objective directly in front of her, gleaming at the top of the hill like a beacon in the soft twilight dimness. Janna's first impression of the mansion the gossip columns sometimes referred to as Santine's Castle was that it didn't look like a castle at all. The massive residence, with its red-shingled roof and honey-beige stone, looked far more like a stately old Spanish monastery. There was even a belltower. She supposed she shouldn't have been surprised that the media hadn't drawn the same simile as she. Santine's risqué reputation didn't bring to mind thoughts of monasteries or the chaste life. Whatever the man's morals, she couldn't fault his taste in real estate. The mansion shone in the lushly landscaped hillside setting like a finely crafted jewel. And she hadn't the slightest doubt that jewel would be very carefully guarded.

A twelve-foot brownstone wall appeared to encircle the estate, and there was a decorative, black-grilled main entrance that was guarded by a gatehouse fronting the road. She knew the futility of applying at the gatehouse for entrance, and drove slowly past the mansion until she rounded a curve in the road. Then she quickly pulled into a small stand of trees beside the road and shut off the engine. She drew a deep breath as she stared at the brownstone wall before her. The walls of Jericho couldn't have appeared more impregnable to her at that moment, and she certainly had no horn to blow to send it tumbling to the ground.

Then she gave herself an admonishing shake and opened the door and got out of the car. She might not have a horn, but she did have a rope and grappling hook in the trunk of the car. She hadn't expected it to be easy to breach the estate grounds.

She supposed she should be grateful that it was a stone wall, where she could at least find hand- and toe-holds in the rough surface. She slammed the car door and strode briskly toward the trunk of the Chevette.

Ten minutes later she was sitting triumphantly on the top of the wall, swiftly changing the grappling hook to the other side of the wall. It only took her a few minutes to climb down the rope into the actual estate grounds. She released the rope, absently rubbing her stinging palms on her khaki-covered thighs, and knew a surge of renewed confidence at this victory over the first of the obstacles that she might encounter. That hadn't been so bad. Now to find her way through these woods to the house, and try to find an entrance that wasn't guarded by a disciple as efficient as that dragon of a secretary in Santine's San Francisco office.

She set off quickly through the woods in what she assumed was the general direction of the main residence. She soon stumbled on what appeared to be a bridle path, and after that the going was much faster. She was mentally congratulating herself on the oil-smooth success of her first attempt at trespassing—well, breaking and entering really—when her self-satisfaction was shattered by a sound that caused her to stop dead in her tracks with a shiver of primal fear.

It was the high shrill yelping of dogs that had brought her to a halt. Guard dogs! Why hadn't she realized that there would be guard dogs protecting an estate the size of Santine's? It was a fairly common security measure these days. They obviously had her scent, because she heard a crashing through the underbrush ahead that brought her heart to her throat. She would have rather faced a wild tiger than a trained guard dog. Ever since she was a small child she had possessed a power over animals that she'd always accepted as perfectly natural. There seemed to be a cord of communication that linked her in a bond of empathy so that at times she felt as if she could actually feel their emotions as her own. But facing a ferocious dog that had been taught by man to maim and kill was a different proposition entirely. How could she be sure instinct would triumph over training?

Well, she was soon going to find out, she thought grimly, as two huge Dobermans burst through the underbrush, their white, razor-sharp teeth gleaming as they snarled ferociously. Janna swiftly dropped to the ground, crossing her legs tailor fashion, trying to clear her mind of all fear, and watched the Dobermans racing toward her.

Rafe Santine gazed broodingly into his brandy, occasionally swirling the amber liquid in the cut-crystal glass. The forty-year-old Courvoisier was rare and, obviously, very expensive, but it might have been wood alcohol, for all the enjoyment he was receiving from it. His face darkened in a forbidding frown. The brandy was as tasteless and boring as everything else in his life at the moment. He took another sip and then lowered the glass, uttering an impatient obscenity that was a souvenir of his early years as a construction foreman. If he wasn't careful, he'd be drinking himself into a stupor from sheer boredom, and he'd never needed that kind of crutch. He'd always had a keen zest for life and the games that he'd played so expertly. He found the manipulations involved in big business as exciting as high-stakes poker.

Why, after twenty years of loving every minute of that challenge, was it suddenly beginning to pall? It must be this damn flu bug that he'd picked up three months ago. He'd probably be himself again in no time, once he was back in harness, provided he didn't go crazy with this blasted inactivity first. For the thousandth time he cursed his own arrogant stubbornness, which had led him to ignore the doctor's orders and continue to work his usual fourteen-hour days while he was fighting off the virus.

He'd been furiously indignant when his body, which had always accepted every demand he placed on it, betrayed him in this instance and he collapsed and had to be hospitalized with severe bronchitis. Now he wouldn't be able to return to work for another two months. Two months! He had only been in Carmel for a week, and boredom was already scraping like sandpaper on a temper that wasn't known to be placid under the best of conditions.

He gazed impatiently around at the book-lined mahogany walls and the magnificent red-and-cream Persian carpet that covered the gleaming parquet floors. Then he scowled critically at the long leather couch and easy chair that fronted the massive stone fireplace at the far end of the room. He should have the house redecorated during his enforced stay at the estate. It would give him something to do other than twiddle his thumbs for the next couple of months. He frowned moodily and sipped at his brandy thoughtfully. No, damn it, he liked the Castle just as it was. The problem with having unlimited means to get exactly what you wanted was that, once the dream was a reality, there was nowhere to go from there.

There was a polite knock on the library door, before Pat Dawson strolled into the room with a white folder in his hands and a sunny smile on his boyish face. Santine regarded him sourly as he came toward him. As incredibly efficient as his young assistant had proved to be, he didn't know if he'd be able to tolerate that wholesome *joie de vivre* for an entire two months. Dawson just might find himself sent scurrying back to San Francisco to act as a liaison between Santine and the various conglomerates under his dominion.

"Sorry to disturb you," Dawson said smoothly, ignoring Santine's moody glare as if it didn't exist.

He paused to turn on the desk light. "It's getting dark earlier every day now," he commented as he stopped beside the high-backed leather chair where Santine was inelegantly sprawled. "Did you notice that some of the leaves are beginning to turn?"

"No, I didn't notice," Santine growled, frowning at him ferociously. "Is that what you wanted to tell me?"

Dawson raised an eyebrow at Santine's sarcasm. Lord, the man was in a savage humor these days. "No, that was just chitchat," he replied calmly, opening the file folder and drawing out several invoices. "I thought I'd get your okay before I sent a check for these little pretties," he said with a genial grin. He placed the invoices on the Sheraton table beside Santine's chair. "They're a bit exorbitant even for Miss Simmons's expensive tastes."

Santine picked up the bills and carelessly rifled through them. "Diane is getting greedy," he said expressionlessly. He tossed the invoices back on the table and took a long swallow of his drink, before he ordered tersely, "Pay them."

Dawson nodded as he gathered up the bills and put them back into the folder. "Right. I just thought you should see them."

Santine smiled cynically. "I'm a very rich man, Pat, and rich men are expected to pay for their pleasures." He stood up lazily and strode over to the portable bar across the room and refilled his glass. "I couldn't expect luscious little Diane to accommodate me without suitable compensation, could I? She wouldn't understand an arrangement without a monetary foundation."

There was a mocking cynicism in Santine's face that caused a speculative flicker in Dawson's eyes. Did Santine really believe his only attraction for the women who flocked around him was the massive size of his bank account? Pat dismissed the thought at once. There was no vestige of false modesty in

Santine's makeup. He knew down to the last degree the extent of every asset he possessed, and he was far from shy about admitting it to anyone. He had to be well aware of the sexual magnetism he exerted over women. Since he'd become Santine's personal assistant over a year ago, Dawson had acted as a bulwark more times than he could remember, to shield Santine from dealing with his discarded mistresses. Some had been frankly avaricious, but there had been others who seemed to be sincerely infatuated with the tycoon.

What was it that drew them to Santine like a moth to a flame? The man wasn't really good-looking, he thought impersonally as he watched Santine stride back over to his easy chair and drop into it, propping his feet indolently on the hassock. He was far from the matinée-idol type, who was supposed to be every woman's dream. In those casual black suede pants and charcoal-gray crew-neck sweater, he looked more like a longshoreman than a sophisticated rake who probably knew his way around more bedrooms than Don Juan had in his prime. His large frame measured in at almost six foot four, and at first glance he gave the impression of being slightly overweight. But there was not an ounce of fat on that massive body. From the brawny shoulders to the strong columns of his thighs, he was as finely honed as a razor-sharp machete.

Machete. Dawson's lips quirked at the aptness of the simile. Santine did remind him of that bold, dangerous weapon. Those blunt, craggy features should have been ugly, but they weren't. Instead, the Slavic width of his cheekbones and the bold, thrusting chin were lent a certain fascination by the underlying strength and power in that face. Even the thick black eyebrows couldn't overshadow the piercing challenge in the darkness of Santine's eyes and the sensuality and slight cruelty in the curve of his lips. Yes, Santine was no delicate subtle Toledo blade, but a slashing, curving scimitar that would carve a path ruthlessly through any opposition.

Not that Santine couldn't be as subtle and manipulative as a veritable Machiavelli when he chose. More often than not, however, Santine didn't choose to clothe that iron fist in a velvet glove but used his economic power and dynamic personality to bludgeon his antagonists into smithereens. Perhaps this was the secret of his attraction for women. Besides that almost overpowering virility, he radiated an aura of power and leashed danger obviously very intriguing to certain types of women.

Santine's lips twisted mockingly as he caught Dawson's speculative stare. "You shouldn't disapprove of my indulging Miss Simmons's hunger for trinkets," he said silkily. "I assure you, she'll earn every one of them before these two months are over."

"It's none of my business, Mr. Santine," Dawson said quietly. "I wouldn't presume to question your private affairs. I just thought that you should see these particular bills."

"You're right, it's none of your business, Pat," Santine said curtly, finishing the second brandy in one swallow and crashing the glass down on the table beside him. Then he sighed and ran his fingers through his heavy dark hair. "God," he said wearily, "I'm sorry, Dawson. You were quite right to question it. I would have torn a strip off you if you hadn't."

Santine's apology surprised Dawson more than his former rudeness. His employer's bluntness and lack of tact were well known, but he'd never heard him apologize to anyone in all the time he'd worked for him. His lips pursed in a soundless whistle. This new volatility could be as dangerous to handle as nitroglycerine. "It's understandable that you'd be annoyed, Mr. Santine," he said carefully, "I never meant . . ." He stopped as he was interrupted by the shrill ringing of the phone on the massive mahogany desk. He looked at Santine inquiringly, and the older man made an impatient gesture for him to get it. "It's the house phone," he commented as he picked up the receiver and announced briefly, "Dawson."

Santine proceeded to ignore Dawson's murmured phone conversation and continued staring moodily down at his empty brandy glass. Whatever it was, Pat could handle it. There were certainly no world-shaking decisions to be made at this hellishly boring Shangri-la by the sea.

It seemed that Dawson didn't agree with him, for he looked up at that moment, covering the receiver with his hand. "It's Sal Goldsmith, head of security, Mr. Santine. It seems that we have a trespasser."

Santine looked up sharply. "Why the hell are they bothering me with that?" he asked. "Goldsmith has been handling trespassers and thieves without consulting me for years."

Dawson's lips quirked in amusement. "He's puzzled about exactly what to do with this particular trespasser," he said solemnly, his blue eyes twinkling. "He finds the situation a bit unusual."

Santine's eyes narrowed. "Unusual?"

Dawson nodded. "The intruder came over the wall using a rope and a grappling hook. The video camera picked up the breach immediately, and security turned loose the dogs."

Santine grimaced. "I can see why the situation is unusual," he said dryly. "Are there any pieces left to send to the hospital?"

"Some very nice ones, according to Sal." Dawson grinned, "And in quite excellent health, at that. When he and Jackson intercepted her as she was approaching the house, both of the Dobermans were frolicking at her heels like lap dogs. She even had to restrain them from attacking Goldsmith when he grabbed her."

"She?" Santine asked alertly. "Our trespasser is a woman?"

"A very attractive one," Dawson replied, leaning back in the leather executive chair. "And very determined, I would say. Climbing that wall would be no easy task for any ordinary woman, even with a rope. It's over twelve feet high."

"How did she get around the dogs?" Santine asked softly, his eyes narrowed in thought. "She couldn't have been carrying raw meat, I suppose."

Dawson shook his head. "The first thing guard dogs are taught is to eat only out of their own bowls, for that very reason."

"Interesting," Santine said slowly. "Very interesting. Was she carrying any weapons?"

"Not even a hat pin," Dawson answered. "Sal says that she went to all this trouble just to speak to you."

Santine smiled cynically. "Well, it's an unusual approach, anyway. Didn't anyone tell her that I already have a mistress in residence at the moment?"

"It probably wouldn't make any difference to someone as determined as our intruder," Dawson said flippantly. "Anyone who could scale a twelve-foot wall would snap her fingers at another woman."

"Perhaps you're right at that," Santine drawled. "She certainly doesn't appear to be shy about going after what she wants. It's a quality that I admire."

"What shall I tell Goldsmith to do with her?" Dawson asked. "He wants to know if he should call the Sheriff's Department."

Santine was silent for a long moment, before a smile touched his lips. "No, I think not. Persistence like that shouldn't go unrewarded. Tell Goldsmith to bring her to the library. I'll see what the lady has to offer."

Dawson shrugged, and spoke rapidly into the phone. "He'll bring her right over; it'll only be a few moments," he said as he replaced the receiver.

"Where is she?" Santine asked idly. He was really in bad shape to become so intrigued by the appearance of an ambitious little hooker who looked on him as her next target. But how in the hell had she gotten around those Dobermans?

"Across the courtyard in the security office," Dawson replied, watching curiously as Santine stood up and strolled lazily to the window overlooking the tiled courtyard. The floodlights had been turned on, giving a daylight clarity to the scene. Dawson also got to his feet and joined Santine at the window, his eyes on the three people rapidly approaching the house.

"She's quite tall," he commented casually as he distinguished the feminine form between the two security guards.

Santine's gaze was also fixed absorbedly on the woman. "Yes," he agreed absently. "But look at the way she moves. I've never seen a woman so graceful."

"You think she may be worth your time after all, then?" Dawson asked, his brow arched quizzically.

There was a strange flicker in the depths of Santine's black eyes as he said slowly, his gaze still on the woman's khaki-clad form, "There's a distinct possibility, Pat. There's definitely a distinct possibility."

Two

"Thanks, Sal, you can go now. I'll handle it from here," the young man behind the desk said genially as he appraised Janna with frank curiosity. "When a decision is made in regard to the Sheriff's Department, I'll let you know."

The two burly security men nodded in respectful acquiescence and quietly left the room, and Janna took a step closer to the desk with an eagerness she couldn't conceal. The quiet luxury of the library could be dimly discerned, illuminated as it was by just the one desk lamp; but surely she'd been taken to see Mr. Santine himself. Then she felt her hopes plummet as she got a better look at the man leaning lazily back in the executive chair.

This couldn't be Santine. Even though the security men were treating him with deference, there was no way the man behind the desk could be the ruthless legend that was Rafe Santine. There was nothing forceful or intimidating about this young man, with his modishly cut acorn-brown hair and appealing blue eyes. Had she gone through all this trouble just to be relegated to one of Santine's underlings?

"You're not Mr. Santine," Janna accused flatly, disappointment making her tone imperious. "I want to see Mr. Santine."

"And so you shall." The deep voice was a curious blend of sandpaper on velvet and came from the dark shadows beside the long window at the far end of the room. "Let's have some light on the subject, Pat. I want a better look at her."

"Right, Mr. Santine." The blue-eyed man at the desk pressed a button on a console, and the room suddenly flared into light.

Santine. Janna's eyes widened as the man strolled toward them with casual grace not usually found in a man so large. She was vaguely conscious of thick dark hair worn a trifle long, a blunt, almost Slavic face, and eyes so black and piercing that they sent a shiver through her. But that wasn't what caused her suddenly to catch her breath and experience an odd sensation of weakness. Santine radiated a power and virility that seemed to dominate his surroundings effortlessly. For the first time in her life, Janna felt a strange sense of being threatened by another human being.

Threatened? Ridiculous! How could Santine be a threat to her? All he could do was say no to her pleas, and she would leave and never see him again. It must be the tension and turmoil of the evening that was making her so stupidly imaginative.

"Very nice," Santine said silkily, his gaze moving over her almost caressingly. "Not beautiful, but definitely arresting. Don't you think so, Pat?" He half leaned, half sat on the corner of the desk.

"She's lovely," the brown-haired man agreed politely.

Janna felt as if she were on an auction block, as Santine continued to appraise her with an intimacy that caused the color to rise to her cheeks. She firmly brushed away the unusual shyness that threatened to overcome her. "Mr. Santine, I'm very sorry to have had to approach you in this manner," she said quietly, her eyes fixed earnestly on his face. "I've been trying to arrange an appointment with you for over two weeks. I was getting desperate, or I'd never have resorted to invading your privacy. My name is Janna Cannon."

Santine's lips curved in a mocking smile. "By all means, let us observe the amenities," he said softly, his gaze running keenly over each feature of her face, so that she felt he must be cataloguing them. "This is my assistant, Pat Dawson, and you obviously are well aware of who I am. As for your rather unusual approach, I find it just as intriguing as you obviously meant me to. I enjoy aggression on the part of the woman occasionally. You might remember that."

Janna gazed at him in puzzlement. "Aggression? I didn't mean to appear aggressive, Mr. Santine," she said earnestly. "It's just that time is running out, and it was terribly important that I see you before our deadline is reached. They'll be taking over in two weeks, and we can't allow that to happen."

"A takeover?" Santine drawled, his eyes narrowing. "So you're not working on your own initiative." His lips curved wryly. "You've been sent to persuade me to save your company from a takeover." His gaze once more traveled over her from head to toe with that burning intimacy. "Well, I can't say that I haven't been offered similar inducements before, but this time I might be tempted to agree. You're quite an unusual type, Janna Cannon."

Janna's eyes widened in surprise as she finally realized what he thought her. "I think there's some misunderstanding," she said softly. "I haven't come to offer you what you seem to think, Mr. Santine. In fact I haven't come to offer you anything at all. I'm here to ask you to contribute a rather large tract of property you own to a very good cause."

There was an odd flicker in the depths of Santine's eyes. "You're rather an unconventional charity canvasser, Miss Cannon," he said softly. "But I must admit you've caught my interest. What property am I to deed to your splendid cause?"

"You own eighteen hundred acres about eighty miles southwest of Los Angeles," Janna replied, her

brown eyes grave. "We need that property desperately,
Mr. Santine."

"Pat?" Santine fired at his assistant, without taking his eyes off Janna.

"She must be referring to the tract owned by your
Camino Real Estate subsidiary," Dawson supplied
briskly. "It's been scheduled for a commercial devel-
opment early next year." He paused. "You recently
turned down an offer in the area of two million
dollars for it."

Janna could feel a sinking sensation in her stomach. Though she realized that California real estate
was exorbitantly expensive, she'd had no idea that
this particular property was so valuable.

Santine darted an amused glance at Dawson. "And
you thought Diane was expensive," he murmured
wryly. His gaze returned to Janna with a lingering
amusement. "I'm curious to know why you think I'd
turn over a valuable piece of real estate to you out
of the goodness of my heart. I hadn't realized that
I'd acquired the reputation of being quite such a
philanthropist."

There was a sound from Dawson that was halfway
between a snort and a delicate cough. "Sorry," he
said solemnly.

"Pat doesn't share your views, evidently," Santine
said dryly. "And he knows me better than a good
many people. Doesn't that discourage you, Miss
Cannon?"

It did, but she couldn't let him know that. "I can't
afford to be discouraged, Mr. Santine," she murmured. "We must have that land."

"That's a sizable piece of property," he said cynically. "You do think big, Miss Cannon. Tell me, what
worthy organization do you represent?"

"We're going to need every acre," she said solemnly.
"It's not greed, but necessity, that's driving me to
you. I'm a game warden and curator at a wild-animal
reserve near San Diego. Our lease has been broken,

and we have only another two weeks before we'll have to start rounding up the animals and shipping them to zoos if we can't find another home for them." Her lips tightened resolutely. "I'm not going to let that happen."

"A wild-animal reserve," Santine said slowly. "Yes, you would need a large amount of acreage for that. But why *my* land?"

"The climate in that area is mild and the terrain basically what the animals are accustomed to at our own reserve," Janna replied eagerly. "It's very important that they not be exposed to any abrupt or radical changes. Your property would be ideal."

"How kind of you to say so," Santine said ironically. He strolled over to a huge brown leather easy chair and dropped into it, stretching his legs out lazily in front of him on the matching ottoman. "And why is it so important that these specimens have no shocks to their fragile psyches?"

Ignoring the mockery in his face, Janna answered swiftly. "Because we're dealing primarily with endangered species. The reason Professor Sandler first established the reserve was to provide a natural environment to encourage the breeding potential of several species of wildlife that refused to reproduce in captivity. If we can't find a way of persuading them to mate, there's a very real possibility that they may soon be extinct."

"How regrettable," Santine said coolly, his impenetrable gaze fixed on her face that was now alight with passion. "It seems to mean a great deal to you, but I don't see how you can expect me to share your enthusiasm. I can't say that I've ever been overly fond of animals." One thick dark brow arched mockingly. "I've never even kept one as a pet."

"You don't have to be sentimental over animals to admit that we have a duty to preserve them," she argued desperately. "If you believe that Darwin's theory of evolution was essentially correct, then you must believe that we have a responsibility to encourage the evolution of our fellow species. If you believe that God put us in the Garden of Eden for a purpose, then you must know that it's the gravest of sins to kill off our companions in that garden. Either way, we have a moral obligation that can't be denied."

"That very neatly covers all the bases," Santine drawled, a glint of admiration in his eyes. "And very eloquently put, too. Your Professor Sandler is obviously a wise gentleman."

"He's quite brilliant and completely dedicated," Janna said simply. "You couldn't ask for anyone finer to head a project like this. He'd be happy to come and detail our plans for the new reserve in depth with you."

"That's not necessary. I'm quite content with his deputy," Santine said, a tiny frown creasing his brow. "Your professor seems to inspire a surprising amount of devotion in his employees. He must be quite a man."

Janna nodded eagerly. "Yes, he's really wonderful, and so worried about the closing of the reserve. We're staying at a motel in town. May I call him and tell him that you're at least considering contributing the land?"

Santine gazed at her for a long moment, his dark eyes veiled and thoughtful. "Yes, I think you could say that I'm considering your request, Miss Cannon." There was a shocked exclamation from a stunned Pat Dawson, and Santine turned to give him a mocking smile. "It's not all that insane, Pat," he drawled. "Remember, it will be tax-deductible. In my income bracket, I need all the deductions and shelters I can arrange, according to my accountants." Then, as Dawson continued to stare at him with his mouth agape, he ordered briskly, "Why don't you run along to your office and give this Professor Sandler a call? Tell him that Miss Cannon and I are discussing the terms of my contribution."

Dawson rose swiftly to his feet, his face wiped clear of all expression. "Yes, sir. I'll take care of it right away, Mr. Santine." He turned to Janna. "If you'll furnish me with the phone number, Miss Cannon?"

She obediently fumbled in the pocket of her khaki slacks for the paper with David's number on it and put it into Dawson's outstretched hand, her dazed eyes still fixed in wonderment on Santine's expressionless face. "It's room 26B," she said automatically.

After all the heartrending anxiety they'd had about their problems, was the solution going to be as easy as this? Rafe Santine waved his magic scepter and suddenly everything was resolved. She was vaguely conscious of Dawson's swift withdrawal, as the library door closed softly behind him. "You're going to give it to us," she whispered, feeling almost ill with relief. "You're actually going to do it?"

"I didn't say that," he replied coolly. "I said that I'd consider it." He took his feet off the ottoman and pushed it away from him with one foot. "Now, come here and sit down and tell me why I should give you a gift worth more than two million dollars."

Janna felt her hopes deflate as rapidly as they'd risen. Of course it wasn't going to be that simple. No hardheaded businessman of Santine's stamp was going to release that much money without considerably more discussion and probing than he'd done as yet. She moved slowly across the room and dropped gracefully down on the ottoman in front of him.

"I don't know what else to say to you," she admitted hesitantly, her brown eyes wide and solemn in a face that was suddenly a shade paler. "I can only appeal to your kindness and generosity. Besides the essential issue of saving the endangered species, without your help these animals will lose their freedom and have to go back to a life behind bars." Her face was shadowed with pain at the thought.

He was studying her with cool calculation. "I think

that matters to you even more than the other," he observed impersonally. "You detest the idea of your precious four-footed friends in cages, don't you?"

She nodded, her gaze dropping. "I hate to see anything caged," she admitted softly, her voice passionately intense. "I couldn't stand to see them go back to that after living free."

"I see," Santine said slowly, his dark gaze running over her with a curiously searching glance. "I'd wager you're a great deal like your charges in that love for freedom. You're rather like a young wild thing yourself, Miss Cannon."

Janna's eyes flew up to meet his, and she felt her heart give a queer flutter as they encountered their dark intensity. "I don't think it's really important what I am or how I feel," she said huskily, moistening her lips nervously. "It's the wildlife reserve we should be discussing."

"But I don't want to discuss the wildlife reserve at the moment," he said arrogantly. "If I know Dawson, he'll be stripping your brilliant professor of every scrap of information he possesses, on the chance that I might want it." His lips curved cynically. "A very ambitious young man, Dawson."

"He seems very pleasant," Janna said noncommitally, trying to inch away unobtrusively from his overpowering nearness. It was strange that though they weren't even touching she should feel this sensation of being trapped and held. It was as if the heat and vitality emanating from him were reaching out and enfolding her in a velvet webbing.

"Sit still," he ordered tersely, his face darkening in a frown. "I'm sure you're not generally a fidgeter. You have a tranquility about you that's very appealing, in this high-powered world we live in."

She obediently was still and tried to smile. "I suppose I'm a bit uneasy," she admitted simply, gazing at him with a steady frankness. "I don't know what you want from me, Mr. Santine."

"I'll get around to that in time," he said impatiently. "Right now I want to know all about you. Since you're a petitioner at my gates, I'd indulge my little whim if I were you."

It was a far from subtle threat. The man was obviously used to getting his own way, and for some reason it pleased him to display a curiosity about one Janna Cannon. He was quite right. Under the circumstances she mustn't antagonize Santine unduly, if simply satisfying his curiosity would placate him.

"What do you want to know?"

"Everything," he said succinctly, leaning back in his chair and regarding her with narrowed eyes. "You can start with your background."

She shrugged. "I'm afraid you'll be quite bored, Mr. Santine. There's nothing in the least exotic about my life. I was born and raised on a farm in Oklahoma. My mother died when I was three, and my father just before I graduated from high school. My only living relative is my grandmother, who still lives on the farm. I've always wanted to work with animals, and I attended the University of Oklahoma, majoring in zoology. I worked my way through school by taking jobs at zoos around the country during the summer and as a veterinarian's assistant during the school year. After I graduated, I went to work immediately for Dr. Sandler."

"Very concise and to the point," Santine drawled mockingly. "All the facts without really revealing anything about yourself. But then, I rather expected that." He leaned forward suddenly, startling her. "Because opening up to me would have violated your sense of personal freedom, wouldn't it, Janna?"

She felt a little frisson of fear run through her. How had Santine realized that about her in the short time they'd been together? Those dark eyes were fixed on her with catlike intentness, and she had the odd feeling he could see right through the barricade of reserve she'd built around herself. "None of us likes to have our privacy invaded," she said defensively. "I'm sure you don't yourself, Mr. Santine."

"You're right. I hate it," he admitted silkily. "But then, I've reached a position where I don't have to stand for it any more, while you're still vulnerable. Very vulnerable." He repeated those last words with a thoughtfulness that had a trace of underlying satisfaction in it. He suddenly reached out and touched the curve of her cheek. "You have incredibly beautiful bones," he commented absently. "Very unusual."

"My grandmother is a full-blooded Cherokee Indian," Janna said quietly, forcing herself to sit still under that curiously gentle touch. It was almost completely impersonal, so why did she feel as if her skin were burning beneath his fingers?

"Interesting," Santine said softly, his hand dropping away from her face to linger on the thick, lustrous brown braid that nestled on the curve of her breast. He slowly leaned back once again in his chair. "Then that aversion to captivity is probably inherent, which would only make it stronger. I'm making progress."

"Progress?" Janna asked warily, her brown eyes fixed on him with the fear of a gazelle that suddenly senses danger.

"You're something of a challenge, Janna," Santine drawled. "I can't remember ever being so intrigued with a woman before. I suppose it's that skittish, wild aura about you that arouses all my aggressive hunting instincts." His voice dropped to a silken murmur. "You see, I'm not at all like you. I have no scruples about capturing and caging my quarry if it pleases me to do so."

She could feel the color rush to her cheeks as bewilderment and panic surged through her. "It's probably the unconventional way I dropped into your life," she offered desperately. "I'd probably bore you to tears in no time."

He chuckled in sheer enjoyment. "No, you wouldn't

bore me," he said wryly. "Do you realize this is the first time that I've ever had a woman try to talk me out of an attraction for her? A relationship with you might be a little chastening to my ego, but it wouldn't be boring."

Janna leaped to her feet and began to pace back and forth. "We're not a bit alike," she protested. "I might amuse you now, but it wouldn't be long before I'd get on your nerves. If you do feel this so-called attraction for me, it will vanish in the twinkling of an eye."

"God, I love to watch you move," he said absently, his eyes on her pacing figure. "It's sheer music to the senses." Then his glance zeroed in on her face, and it was anything but vague. "I don't expect that you'll amuse me for long," he said bluntly. "I grow bored easily these days. However, you may serve your purpose for the time that I'm in Carmel."

She paused in her pacing to turn and face him. "Just what are you saying to me?" she asked slowly. "I'm afraid I'm a little confused. One moment we're speaking of the wildlife reserve and the next you're giving me the impression that I'm first in line for the position of your next mistress."

"The two aren't as unrelated as you might think," Santine said coolly. "You said you were appealing to my kindness and generosity. I think I possess a modicum of the latter, but I'm sadly lacking in the former. Unless you have something to trade, I'm afraid I wouldn't be interested in your proposition regardless of the tax write-off angle." He paused significantly before ending softly, "Fortunately, you do possess something that I want."

"Sex?" she inquired clearly, her face as composed as his own.

"I haven't decided about that," he said slowly. "It's a distinct possibility sex will play a major role in my plans for you. I haven't thought that far ahead yet." There was an odd restlessness in his eyes as they moved over her face, as if he were searching for something. "Hell, I don't know," he said wearily. "The only thing I'm sure about is that I'm stuck here 'resting' until the doctor gives me the okay to go back to work. I'll go crazy if I don't have something to distract me."

"And I'm to provide that distraction?" Janna asked quietly. She supposed she should be indignant that he would calmly assume she'd let him use her as a toy to beguile away his boredom. Perhaps she might have been but for the importance of the issue at stake.

He nodded briskly, and the smile he gave her was grim. "I said that I'd never had a pet. Well, I've decided to acquire one for the next month or so. My own wild thing to keep me amused until I can return to San Francico."

"And then you'll let me go and turn the property over to Professor Sandler?" Janna asked huskily. She felt that she was in a wild, disjointed dream where nothing made sense but everything was frighteningly real. She shook her head as if to clear it.

Santine evidently mistook her confusion for negation, for his manner took on a ruthlessness that had been absent formerly. "I'd think twice before refusing me, Janna," he said, a thread of steel in his voice. "I'm a very dangerous man to cross, and I make a habit of getting what I want. At the moment I happen to want to cage and hold you for my own for a time." His voice dropped to a silky murmur. "It's either a very luxurious captivity for you for two months or a more permanent one for your precious four-footed friends. The choice is yours."

"You're giving me very little option," Janna said tautly. "You know that I could never bear the alternative."

"Yes, I do know that. So I trust you're acceding to my terms?" She nodded reluctantly, and he continued incisively. "Shall we clarify the proposition? You agree to stay with me until I return to San Francisco, in any capacity that I require of you. In return, I'll deed the property over to the wildlife reserve immediately, with a cancellation option that I can exercise any time in the next two months if you prove unsatisfactory."

"It's a very biased agreement," Janna said dryly. "It puts you in a position of supreme power and leaves me with absolutely no protection against you."

"Which is exactly the way I like it," he said, appearing supremely composed. "While you're with me, I want you totally at my disposal. I don't want you in communication with your wonderful professor or any of your friends. You're not to phone anyone or attempt to see them without my permission."

"A cage indeed," Janna said dryly. "Don't you think you're being a trifle unreasonable?"

"Not for two million dollars," Santine retorted promptly. "Do you agree?"

"With one reservation," she said quietly. "I place a call home to my grandmother every three days. I won't relinquish that privilege."

He shrugged. "I'll accept that," he said casually. "I'll send my driver to pick up your luggage at the motel. You'll stay here tonight."

"May I ask if I'll be expected to occupy your bed tonight?" she asked with a coolness she was far from feeling.

His eyes narrowed on her face. "What if I said yes?" he asked curiously. "You know that I'm leaving myself the option of demanding it of you at my pleasure? Would you be willing to sell yourself for this idealistic project of yours?"

Janna flinched involuntarily at the callousness of his phrasing. Then she drew a deep breath and tilted her chin determinedly. "Yes, if you insist," she said simply. "That particular commodity has been sold for less valuable prices than the preservation of an entire species. This isn't Victorian times, where a simple biological coupling would be considered a fate worse than death. It won't change what I think or what I am. Afterward I'll be able to walk away without a single look back."

"You do like to throw challenges at me, don't you? I just might be tempted to prove you wrong, doe eyes." He stood up, moved swiftly toward the desk and pressed a button on the console. "But not tonight. If I feel any lascivious urges, I have a very accomplished lady in residence to satisfy me."

Janna's knees felt weak with relief, but she was careful not to let it show in her expression. "As you like," she said composedly. "You needn't have my bags picked up. I have to return my rental car anyway. I'll pick up my overnight case and speak to David at the same time."

But Santine was shaking his head adamantly. "I'll have Dawson tell your professor that you're staying here to help iron out the legal technicalities of the property transfer," he said curtly. "I want you here tonight. I'll have your car returned for you. Where did you park it?"

"I'm not sure," Janna said vaguely. "It's in a stand of trees outside the wall. It's a blue Chevette."

"Oh yes, the wall," Santine said thoughtfully, his lips quirking. "That was quite a stunt." His eyes ran over her. "You must be stronger than you look."

She nodded. "I'm quite strong. After growing up on a farm and then working at the game reserve, it would be unusual if I weren't."

"And what magic did you use on the Dobermans?" he asked quizzically, leaning lazily against the desk. "You can't say that wasn't unusual. They should have torn you apart."

She smiled, her face gentle. "Most animals like me," she said simply. "We understand one another."

"There's got to be more to it than that," he said skeptically, his lips curving in a cynical smile.

"Goldsmith said those dogs were ready to attack their own handlers to protect you."

"I can't explain it any more clearly," she said, shrugging helplessly. "Perhaps it's because I'm part Cherokee. Indians have a centuries-old tradition of being in tune with nature. My grandmother says it's not at all unusual for there to be a member of the tribe who has an affinity with animals."

There was a soft tap on the door, before it opened to admit a slight, black-jacketed servant. Santine looked toward him, frowning darkly as if impatient of the interruption. Then he grimaced. "That's right, I did ring for you, didn't I, Fred?" he asked ruefully. "I'm afraid it slipped my mind." He turned to Janna. "We usually breakfast on the terrace at ten. I'll expect you." He gestured toward the servant. "This is Fred Stokley. This is Miss Cannon, Fred. He'll show you to your room." He turned to Stokley and added, "After you've settled her, come back to the study, Fred. I have some instructions for you."

"Yes, Mr. Santine," Fred Stokley said, with majestic dignity. He had the clear, incisive diction of one educated in an English public school, and Janna gazed at him with renewed interest. In his early fifties, Stokley couldn't have been over five foot six, but his royal bearing more than made up for his lack of stature. His pale and rather nondescript face was dominated by a pair of fine gray eyes, which were his one attraction. His light-brown hair, which receded sharply from his broad forehead, also gave the impression of colorlessness.

It was impossible not to be impressed by the warm, glowing beauty of the spacious foyer as she followed Stokley from the library. Under the enormous copper chandelier, the parquet floors shone with the mellow luster of fine polished oak. The chandeliers' masterly wrought Spanish beauty was augmented by the incredible fact that it wasn't electricity but seemingly hundreds of *candles* that lit the beaten copper and cast a magical flicker of light over the entire foyer and staircase area. The staircase itself was equally magnificent; its extravagantly wide rich mahogany steps were carpeted with an exquisite red-and-cream Persian runner of the same pattern that she'd noticed in the library.

They seemed to pass an amazing number of doors along several corridors before Stokley finally paused. "I think you'll find this chamber satisfactory, Miss Cannon," he said augustly as he opened the door and preceded her into the room, flicking on the light switch as he did so.

She would have to be very critical not to be satisfied with a room as lovely as this, Janna thought wryly as she looked around bemusedly. The bedroom was very spacious, and as beautifully decorated as the rest of the house. It was carpeted lushly in a silver blue that contrasted exquisitely with the delicate eyelet drapes and matching eyelet comforter on the king-sized bed. The gleaming mahogany bedside table and the small desk in the corner had the same timeless beauty of fine craftmanship that she'd noticed in the furniture in the library and foyer.

"There's a combination bath and dressing room adjoining," Stokley said crisply, moving to a dark mahogany door on the far side of the room and opening it. He gave the bathroom a cursory glance before returning to where she stood in the center of the room. "I believe everything is in order." He gestured to the elegant cream princess phone on the desk. "If you need anything more, you need only to dial nine, and it will ring in the servants' quarters. Would you like Maria to bring you a meal?"

"No, I had a light supper earlier in the evening, thank you."

"Perhaps some hot chocolate, then?" Stokley persisted politely.

Janna shook her head. "Nothing, thank you. I think I'll just shower and go to bed. I'm a bit tired."

"Very well," Stokley said, moving with regal dignity toward the door. "There's a clock on the bedside table if you wish to set the alarm. Please let me know if we may serve you in any capacity. Good night, Miss Cannon."

Stokley was a butler straight out of a drawing-room comedy, and completely inconsistent with the type of servant she'd have thought a man of Santine's almost aggressive modernity would have chosen. Then Janna's smile slowly faded as she realized that this anomaly only highlighted the complexity of Santine's character. He was obviously a multidimensional man, and his menace was magnified accordingly.

Well, tonight she didn't have to worry about Santine's idiosyncrasies. She would have that shower and dismiss the man from her mind. Tomorrow was time enough to ponder the consequences of the strange bargain she'd made. She strode briskly toward the bathroom, which proved to be almost as large as the bedroom at her cottage on the reserve. It was beautifully decorated in navy-and-white tile, and carpeted in the same silver blue as the bedroom.

Janna stripped off her clothes and stepped into the shower, turning on the faucets to a warm setting. She let the water pour over her in a gentle, soothing cascade, experiencing a long moment of lazy sensual contentment before beginning briskly to soap herself. Five minutes later she was drying herself on a huge white bath towel she had plucked from the warmed rack and congratulating herself on successfully banishing Santine from her thoughts.

As it turned out, she was a little too eager with her self-congratulations. She had no sooner flicked out the bedroom lights and slipped naked between the crisp, scented cotton sheets than thoughts of Santine slipped easily through the barricades she had lifted to keep him out. It was all completely mad. No man who possessed Santine's ruthless pragmatism would hand over two million dollars merely to appease a whim. Yet, incredibly, he had done just that, and she was lying in this luxurious bed in Santine's Castle as living proof of it. He must really be bored to develop such an obsessive interest in her, Janna thought wryly. She supposed she could be considered moderately attractive, but she didn't hold a candle to the ravishing beauties he usually chose as his mistresses.

Perhaps it wouldn't even go that far. No one could say that he was overcome with a raging desire for her, and he'd said that he was keeping a woman here for his pleasure. It was more than likely he would have second thoughts about that aspect of her stay here, once he compared her meager charms to those of his current paramour.

There was no reason for her to feel this threatened by a man she barely knew. Yet an odd shiver ran through her as she remembered how those narrowed dark eyes had seemed mercilessly to strip away all her protective covering, both mental and physical. She had felt more vulnerable than ever before in her life, sitting on that ottoman enmeshed in the web woven by the force of Santine's personality.

It was strange, the effect that he'd had on her. She'd felt an odd, languid weakness in every limb; yet, ambivalently, she'd never felt so zestfully alive. Most peculiar. It must have been that the anxiety and strain of the evening had affected her physical senses to such an extent that she'd magnified the sway that Santine had exerted upon her. She would probably be her usual composed self after a good night's rest. Well satisfied with her reasoning, she plumped up her pillow and firmly willed herself to go to sleep.

Three

Janna awoke, as usual, when the first gray light that preceded the dawn was brightening the sky. For the first time in her life she wished she weren't one of those people who awakened totally aware and alert from the moment they opened their eyes. There was no possibility of going back to sleep no matter how hard she tried, and what was she supposed to do until the ten-o'clock breakfast decreed by Santine? Well, she couldn't bear lying here doing nothing. Perhaps she could while away the hours by exploring the estate.

She tossed the covers aside impatiently and jumped out of bed. As she strode with lithe energy toward the bathroom, she halted in surprise as she saw both her overnight bag and the khaki shirt and slacks set neatly on the Queen Anne chair by the door. The latter had been laundered to pristine freshness, and her suede desert boots, placed with careful precision on the floor by the chair, had also been thoroughly brushed.

Janna shook her head in wonder, her lips curving in an amused smile. There was something curiously magical about the appearance of her possessions in this fashion. She wondered whimsically if Santine's Castle had its own bevy of elves who appeared after everyone was asleep, to whisk everything in order. She wouldn't put it past Santine to be able to command that kind of service.

Still smiling, she unfastened her overnight bag and withdrew fresh underthings and disappeared into the bathroom. She deliberately took as long as she could with her usual morning toilette. She dressed in her khaki outfit once again and returned to the bedroom, pleased to see that the sky was streaked with the glorious lavender and pink of the sunrise. At least she wouldn't be blundering around in the dark and possibly getting the Dobermans set on her again. Though it might not be a bad idea at that, she thought wistfully. She could use a little company on her ramble. She was briefly tempted to find the kennels to release them herself but reluctantly discarded the idea. She had an idea that those grim-faced security men wouldn't be pleased if she made friends with their canine guards. No, she would have to go it alone.

She quietly left the bedroom and went through the silent, slumbering house to the courtyard door, through which she'd been brought last night. Unlocking it, she slipped through the brass-bracketed door, closed it softly behind her, and set off on her tour of exploration.

The estate grounds were just as lovely as the mansion itself, she soon discovered. She toured the estate, from the beige-and-rose mosaic-tiled courtyard, with its graceful fountain, to the charming bridle paths that abounded on the lush, verdant acreage. It was all very impressive, but it wasn't until she emerged from the woods at the top of the cliff that she caught her breath at the sheer magnificence that lay before her.

The cliff fell steeply to the rugged, boulder-strewn beach below and overlooked the wild, crashing glory of the Pacific. There was nothing before her but the stormy primitive restlessness of the white curling waves pounding against the rocks below and the stretch of lonely golden sand that bordered Santine's domain. Standing there with the fresh morning

breeze caressing her cheeks, she felt a joyous exhila-
ration surge through her that had been absent in
her appreciation of the more civilized attractions of
Santine's estate.

It seemed that Santine also enjoyed this particular
view, Janna thought as she climbed slowly up a
slight incline to a redwood gazebo at the very edge of
the cliff. The interior of the gazebo was small and
cozy and was bordered by scarlet-cushioned benches.
There were matching scarlet curtains hanging from
the eaves, caught back by tasseled sashes to permit
the sea breeze to whip through the enclosure with a
very satisfying freedom.

Janna seated herself on the bench closest to the
cliff's edge and leaned her arms on the redwood
wall, gazing out at the sparkling azure waters with a
sigh of contentment. This was much closer to the
wild, primitive beauty that filled her with a sense of
belonging. From this vantage point she could see a
steep rocky path a few hundred yards away that
wound down the cliff to the beach below, but she
wasn't tempted to continue her exploration at the
moment. It was so lovely here that all she wanted to
do was sit and gaze dreamily out over the waters.

She stayed a long time, lost in the peace and
tranquility that flowed into her as the tide flowed
onto the sandy shore so far below her. It was only
when she noticed that the sun was surprisingly high
in the sky that she left the gazebo and slowly returned to the castle. Too slowly, evidently, for she
was met at the courtyard door by a flustered young
Mexican maid in a wine-colored uniform who'd obviously been stationed there to wait for her. "Señor
Santine is waiting for the señorita," she said disapprovingly. "Follow me, *por favor.*"

Janna smothered a smile as she obediently followed the maid through the impressive foyer and
equally magnificent formal living room to the French
doors that led to the terrace. It seemed Santine's

servants weren't accustomed to anyone's treating his wishes with anything but reverent respect. If everyone in the castle behaved similarly, it was no wonder he was so arrogant.

The subject of her uncomplimentary thoughts was sitting, chair pushed back from an elegantly appointed damask-covered table. The alluring, negligee-clad blonde beside him was gazing at him with a cloying adoration not designed to lessen Santine's opinion of himself. Not that Janna could really blame the woman for being physically attracted to Santine. The casual faded jeans he wore only served to emphasize the strong muscular column of his thighs and the hard flatness of his stomach, and the white crew-neck fisherman's sweater not only complimented his virile darkness but made his massive shoulders appear even broader.

The glance he gave her was not nearly as approving when he looked up to see her walking through the French doors. In fact, there was a distinct flicker of annoyance, quickly hidden. "Good morning, Miss Cannon," Santine said, rising lazily to his feet. "You're looking very alert and wide awake this morning. I understand you've been exploring the grounds since daybreak. Security wasn't at all sure you weren't casing the place despite my assurance to the contrary. Do you always get up so early?"

Janna nodded. "Always. There aren't enough hours in the day at the reserve," she said softly. "Though I'd probably do it anyway. I'm definitely a day person."

"While Diane, here, is definitely a night person," he said mockingly, and there was no mistaking the double entendre in his allusion to his blond companion. "Interesting contrast."

For a brief moment Janna felt a twinge of anger at the callous cruelty of the remark. How could Santine's mistress bear the subtle insult in his manner toward her? He seemed to care not a whit if he hurt or embarrassed her. She turned to face the woman seated across from Santine with a warm, sympathetic smile. "I don't believe we've met," she said gently. "I'm Janna Cannon. I'm going to be here for a while, and I hope we'll be friends."

Her smile was met by a blank, surprised stare from eyes that were as blue as a mountain lake. The woman was extraordinarily attractive, Janna thought impersonally. Though quite small, she was endowed with amazingly voluptuous curves, her long, white-blond hair tumbling over her shoulders in a silky curtain. Her face, while not classically beautiful, had the fresh prettiness of a high-school cheerleader.

"How rude of me not to introduce you," Santine said silkily, and she received the subtle impression that he was slightly incensed with her for some reason. "Janna, this is Diane Simmons, a very *close* associate."

"How do you do," Diane murmured, her smile absent, before turning back to Santine with an eagerness she didn't bother to disguise. "It's really quite inexpensive, considering the workmanship involved, Rafe. Do say that I may have it."

"I'll consider it," Santine said noncommittally, his eyes on Janna. "We'll discuss it later. Janna, come and sit down and have some breakfast. You no doubt worked up an appetite, with all your wanderings." He gestured to the chair next to him. "You must have enjoyed the gazebo to stay there so long."

"I loved it," she said enthusiastically, coming forward and slipping into the place he'd indicated. Then a frown of puzzlement creased her brow. "How do you know how long I stayed there?" she asked curiously.

"Oh, Rafe has those video cameras planted all over the estate," Diane said lightly, applying herself to the melon on her plate with dainty greed. "No one can make a move without security's knowing all about it."

"I see," Janna said slowly, feeling strangely deflated.

The wonderful sensation of freedom and peace that she'd known on the cliff this morning had been nothing but a mirage. It was suddenly tainted with the knowledge that she'd been watched all the time by the casual, impersonal eyes of Santine's security force.

Santine's keen gaze was on her revealing face. "You don't like the idea," he observed flatly, his hand reaching for the silver coffeepot beside him and filling her cup.

"No, I don't like it," she agreed quietly, avoiding his eyes. She took a piece of toast and nibbled at it listlessly. "It seems a needless invasion of privacy."

"Perhaps," he said curtly. "But I regard it as necessary, so I'm afraid you'll have to get used to it. It does have the advantage of allowing me to know the location of discourteous guests who fail to show up on time for breakfast."

"I couldn't exactly be put in that classification, could I?" Janna asked softly. "Guests generally have to be invited."

Santine's lips tightened ominously, and the dark eyes were flying storm signals. "You may have gate-crashed my fortress, but I thought I'd more than demonstrated my willingness to allow you to stay."

Diane Simmons looked up from her melon with a tinkling laugh, her face smooth and expressionless as a pretty doll's. "You mustn't mind the cameras," she said cheerfully, her hand reaching out to close affectionately over Santine's. "Rafe assures me there aren't any in the house, and that's all that's important."

Janna looked at Diane's blank, sunny face with startled amazement. It didn't seem possible that the woman had missed the implications and subtle undercurrents that had been taking place in their conversation, but it appeared this was the case.

Santine shook off the blonde's hand impatiently.

"Why don't you run along and go for a swim, Diane?" he suggested bluntly.

She stood up obediently. "Will you be joining me?" she asked, smiling seductively at him. "I bought a brand-new bikini in town yesterday that I want to show you."

"We'll see," he said casually. "I'm sure you're quite beautiful in it."

"It was very nice meeting you, Miss Simmons," Janna said warmly, trying to make up for Santine's offhandedness. "I hope I see you again soon."

"What?" Diane glanced over at her for a vague instant before smiling brightly. "Oh, sure. It was nice meeting you, too." She drifted off in a cloud of pink chiffon draperies.

Santine's lips were quirking as he regarded the bewilderment on Janna's face when she gazed after Diane Simmons. "I'm afraid your efforts at soothing her ruffled feelings are in vain, Janna. She's really too stupid to be angered or hurt by anything but the most blatant insult. You'll find that she's very like a lovely Siamese cat, who only thinks when it's absolutely necessary. Fortunately, with a luscious body like Diane's, that necessity doesn't arise too often."

"You're not being very kind," Janna said disapprovingly. "Surely you owe Miss Simmons at least a semblance of courtesy."

He stared at her in blank incredulity. "My God, I believe you're actually taking me to task," he said. "I don't think anyone's done that since I was fourteen years old."

"Then someone should have done it long ago," Janna said crisply. "You were very rude to Miss Simmons."

"I thought we'd established that I wasn't a kind man," he said, frowning sulkily. "You needn't champion Diane so enthusiastically. She's quite capable of taking care of herself. Before she came to me she was under the protection of a Greek shipping magnate, and before that she was with a British rock star. She may be stupid, but she knows the rules of the game." His lips curved cynically. "And plays it very profitably, I might add."

For a fleeting moment Santine had the guilty, cross expression of a little boy caught with his hand in the cookie jar, and it gave Janna the courage to persist. "That doesn't exempt you from treating her with ordinary courtesy," she said quietly. "Every human being deserves being accorded a modicum of dignity."

Santine's face clouded angrily, his dark eyes flashing stormily. Then, with a suddenness that caught Janna off guard, his forbidding scowl gave way to a broad grin of infinite amusement. Janna gazed in fascination at the amazing difference it made in his face. It was the first time she'd seen him with an expression reflecting anything but grim moodiness or mocking cynicism. Relaxed, he not only looked ten years younger but possessed a devastating attractiveness.

"I don't recall ever being given a lecture on my treatment of a mistress by the prime candidate to succeed her," he said wryly. "I can see that you're going to provide me with a variety of new experiences."

Janna's eyes dropped to her coffee. She'd temporarily forgotten the terms of her stay at Santine's Castle. "But you said you weren't at all sure you'd exercise that particular option," she said lightly. "I rather thought you might have changed your mind entirely by this morning."

"You'll find I very seldom change my mind about anything," Santine said quietly. "I told Dawson to draw up the papers last night. Your professor was walking on air, and he understood perfectly the necessity of your staying here."

"That's more than I do." Janna made a wry face. "I'm not going to prove very entertaining for a man of your tastes, Mr. Santine. We're as different as night and day."

"How do you know what my tastes in women are?" he asked softly, and Janna looked up suddenly to catch a flicker in the darkness of his eyes. "Perhaps I'm ready for a change from the Dianes of the world. Slightly stupid women are comfortable to be around, as they demand nothing but what I want to give them, but they can also be very dull. I have an idea that whatever you'll be to me, it won't be boring, Janna."

Janna felt a nervous shiver run through her, and she lowered her eyes, hurriedly taking another bite of toast. "The bargain stands, then?" she asked huskily.

"It stands," he replied implacably. Then, with a trace of impatience in his voice, he exclaimed, "For God's sake, put that toast down and take something more nourishing. You're so thin you look almost breakable."

Before she could reply, to her amazement he had scooped a helping of fluffy scrambled eggs on her plate as well as three slices of bacon. "Now, eat, damn it."

"But I never have more than toast and coffee for breakfast," she protested, looking down at the plate distastefully. "This is much too much."

"Then it's a wonder you're as healthy as you are," he said tersely, pouring himself a second cup of coffee. "While you're in my charge you'll eat what I tell you to." He smiled grimly. "I may not ever have had a pet, but that doesn't mean I don't know how to care for one."

She looked up, her face mutinous, but, seeing the determination in his, she obediently picked up her fork. "Oh, very well," she said impatiently. "It's not worth arguing about."

The eggs were surprisingly good, she found, and she discovered that she'd worked up more of an appetite on her walk than she had thought. She set about disposing of the food on her plate with a sudden enthusiasm. She looked up as she polished off the last of the bacon, to notice Santine watching her with an expression of smug satisfaction on his face. "I guess it wasn't too much," she admitted sheepishly.

He chuckled, his dark eyes twinkling. "I guess it wasn't," he agreed solemnly. "Would you like something else?"

"No, thank you," Janna said hurriedly. She took a sip of coffee. "The entire estate is incredibly beautiful, but I fell in love with your gazebo. Do you go there often?"

He nodded. "It's my favorite place on the grounds. I thought you'd like it. Most of my guests find the view a bit too primitive for their tastes."

She shook her head in wonder. "How could they? It's absolutely magnificent. I could have stayed there all day."

"You almost did," Santine said wryly. "I was about to send someone to get you, when you made your appearance." He leaned back in his chair and studied her lazily. "Incidentally, I've sent a man down to the animal reserve to pack up your things and bring them here. I've told Stokley that he's to furnish you with a complete wardrobe for your stay, but most women have some sort of memorabilia they like to have with them."

"I don't," Janna said quietly. "I'm afraid your man is going to have a wasted journey. Other than a few articles of clothing, there's nothing at the cottage that I want." Her lips tightened stubbornly. "And I'm certainly not going to accept any new wardrobe from you."

"Yes, you will," he retorted composedly. "I can't expect you to buy the type of clothes that you'll need for your life here. It's part of the deal." He was gazing at her with a piercing calculation that made her feel slightly uncomfortable. "I should have known that you wouldn't be one to be weighed down by an excess of possessions," he said slowly. "Possessions are a subtle captivity in themselves. You wouldn't want to be tied down even to that extent, would you, Janna?"

"Aren't you guilty of reading psychological undertones into every little aspect of my existence?" she asked evasively. "Perhaps it's poverty, and not choice, that dictates my lack of possessions."

"I don't think so," Santine said, his eyes still intent on her face. "I think you'd be content to have nothing but the clothes on your back if the decision were yours." To her relief that too-perceptive gaze shifted to the cup in his hand, and the subject to a more comfortable one for her. "Do you find your quarters satisfactory? I trust that Stokley attended to all your needs."

"My room is perfectly lovely," she replied sincerely, "and Stokley couldn't have been more solicitous." Her lips curved in a bemused smile. "He's really quite impressive, not at all the type of servant whom I'd expect you to employ."

"You think he's too British upper class for a diamond in the rough like me?" he asked, an amused grin on his face. "Actually, you're not too far off the mark. I hired him away from a British duke who's quite close to the throne; Stokley manages all my residences for me." His eyes took on a glint of mischief. "I think he looks on me as the premier challenge of his long and illustrious career. I paid a small fortune for him, and he's worth every penny of it."

"I can see how he would be," she said, smiling at the almost boyish satisfaction on his face. Despite his blunt, abrupt manner, she was finding this side of Rafe Santine strangely appealing. He was like a gruff little boy whose aggressiveness was a mask for his vulnerability. Then she shook her head in amazement at her own foolishness. What had she been thinking? There was nothing in the least vulnerable about Rafe Santine.

"I think you'll approve of Fred's taste," Santine said easily. "Your wardrobe will be delivered late this afternoon. If you need anything else, just tell either him or Dawson and they'll take care of it. I'm giving a formal dinner party for a few business associates and their wives this evening." He grimaced ruefully. "That's the only form of business activity my doctor is sanctioning for me at the moment. I'll expect you downstairs in the living room at eight."

"You want me at your dinner party?" Janna asked, her eyes widening in surprise. "I'd rather not, thank you. I'm not really good at social functions."

His face hardened. "Be there," he ordered tersely. "I don't expect you to entertain anyone but me. You don't have to indulge in the usual chitchat or parlor tricks if you don't want to. I just want to have something restful to look at when I get disgusted with all the bull that will be flying tonight."

"If you feel like that, why entertain them at all?" she asked quietly.

"The game," he answered simply. "It's all a game, with the stakes getting bigger all the time. I may get sick to death of some of the moves, but I never get tired of winning the game. I like to win." He plucked his napkin from his lap and tossed it on the table before rising to his feet. "Some of the guests will be arriving in a few hours by helicopter. I won't expect you to join us at the pool for lunch, but you *will* come down for dinner. Understand?"

"It would be hard not to," she said wryly. "You're a very incisive man, Mr. Santine."

"Rafe," he corrected curtly, and he turned and strode briskly across the terrace. Before he disappeared through the open French doors he looked over his shoulder to say, "I'll have Stokley bring your lunch to your room. Be sure that you eat every bite." He was gone before she could muster a reply.

Her lips were curved in a rueful smile as she slowly rose to her feet. It seemed that Santine's momentary softening was definitely over and he was back to his usual laconic, autocratic self. She sighed morosely as she thought of the evening ahead. It was true she found the kind of dinner party that Santine was planning unutterably boring, and usually avoided such affairs like the plague. Well, he'd given her no choice but to attend this one. Thank heaven he'd excused her from the luncheon that was to precede it. Now all she had to do was to find a way of occupying herself that would keep her discreetly out of Santine's guests' perimeter until it was time to dress for dinner. Perhaps she would go back to the gazebo for a bit and then explore the path that led down to the beach. Her face brightened at the thought, and she set out once again, with an eager, springing step, toward the courtyard door.

The slanting rays of the late-afternoon sun were casting long shadows on the courtyard tiles when Janna returned to the castle. Her khaki pants were rolled up to her knees, her sandy feet bare, and she was swinging her desert boots in one hand. She paused at the fountain in the center of the courtyard to gaze ruefully at her reflection in the water before giving the tousled image in the mirrored surface a playful flick with her hand that scattered crystal drops onto the rose-beige flagstone tiles. Then she threw back her head and laughed with the sheer joy of living.

It had been such a lovely afternoon, wandering along the rock-strewn beach and wading in the surf. She had even built a sand castle in the image of this lovely Spanish mansion. As she sat on the edge of the fountain and swung her feet in the cool water to wash away the dust and sand that clung to her toes, she looked critically at the bell tower. She hadn't gotten that tower quite right in her sand castle, she mused. She hadn't remembered the brass-trimmed shutters on the two windows. She'd have to be more precise next time. She swung her feet out of the water and kicked them vigorously to rid them of excess water before hopping off the rim of the fountain and padding happily toward the courtyard door.

This time she was met by no less a personage than Fred Stokley, who gave her careless, windblown appearance scarcely a glance before saying with stately dignity, "You weren't home for lunch. Mr. Santine was most displeased."

"I wasn't hungry," she said simply, giving him a sunny smile. Even Stokley's august displeasure couldn't ruin her feeling of sublime contentment. "I'll try to be on time for dinner," she promised. "How much time do I have?"

There was a flicker of a smile in Stokley's eyes as he spoke. "A little over an hour. But you should appear at least fifteen minutes early for cocktails. I took the liberty of laying out an appropriate gown."

"Right." Janna nodded, and started across the foyer, her bare feet slapping against the polished parquet tiles. "I'll hurry, Stokley."

"It would definitely be advisable, Miss Cannon," he said dryly, and she could have sworn there was a thread of amusement in the precise British accent.

She did hurry. Her shower, shampoo, and blow-drying took only thirty minutes, though her hair was still a bit damp when she swiftly rebraided it.

Stokley's choice of an evening gown displayed not only superb taste, but amazing insight into her own preferences. The sunshine-yellow gown was fashioned of a silky jersey, which shimmered rather than shone. It was utterly simple, cut in the Greek fashion, leaving one shoulder bare and then falling gracefully to the floor, giving only a hint of the curves it concealed.

The matching yellow satin sandals had only a medium heel, thank goodness. She hadn't had an occasion to wear high heels since her graduation from college, and these would be bad enough.

She took one glance in the full-length mirror before she left the bedroom. Not bad. The bright yellow of the gown made her olive skin appear to glow in silken contrast, and her shining brown braid looked quite appropriate with the gown's classic style. She hesitated a moment, wondering if she should use a touch of lipstick, before deciding firmly against it. Her lips were always a rich, deep pink anyway, and she wouldn't let Santine think that she'd gone to any extra trouble on his behalf.

She still had a few minutes to spare when she left the bedroom and made her way down the long curving staircase to the formal living room. She took a deep breath in the arched doorway before moving as unobtrusively as possible into the room.

The enormous room was carpeted wall to wall in plush, creamy beige carpet that offered a harmonious contrast to the russet-and-chocolate upholstery of the long velvet couch and occasional chairs that were scattered about the room. There were striped cream-and-chocolate throw pillows on the couch and matching striped velvet drapes at the French doors. Though the room was luxuriously elegant, Janna liked it far less than the other rooms in the castle. It lacked the warmth and subtle Spanish touches that gave the other rooms such character. Strange that Santine should choose this formal room to entertain his guests. Or perhaps not so strange, when one came to think about it. Janna had an idea that he was a man who would carefully guard his inner core of privacy with passionate zeal.

There were perhaps twenty people scattered about the room, obviously engaged in the shallow chitchat that Santine had spoken of so scornfully. She heard a woman's high, shrill laugh, and flinched involuntarily. It reminded her of the harsh, abrasive squawk of a parrot.

"There you are, Janna," Santine said silkily, from behind her. "I was wondering when you were going to make an appearance."

She turned to face him, noticing absently how becoming the elegant black tuxedo was on his powerful frame, before her eyes searched his face for the familiar mockery. Surprisingly, she found nothing but amusement and a curious warmth in the expression on his face. "I'm not late," she protested indignantly. "I still have two minutes. Stokley said so."

He chuckled, his eyes dancing. "Well, if Stokley approves, who am I to argue? He's the final word on protocol in my domain." His gaze went over her in lingering approval. "He certainly outdid himself when he chose that gown. You look lovely, Janna."

There was an odd huskiness in his voice that caused a bewildering wave of heat to surge through her. "Thank you," she said faintly, looking desperately around the room for some excuse to escape the intimate intensity of his gaze. She found it in the form of the peacock-splendid Diane Simmons, who was talking to a rotund, gray-haired man. "Miss Simmons looks fantastic in scarlet, doesn't she?" she asked hurriedly. "I thought blondes weren't supposed to wear anything but pastels."

He ignored the comment as blatantly as he was ignoring his mistress. He took Janna's elbow and turned her gently toward a group of men and women in the corner of the room. "I know I promised you that you wouldn't have to mingle, and I'll keep to it," he said softly. "But it would appear odd if I didn't introduce you to a few guests. I'll have Dawson extricate you in a few minutes. Okay?"

Janna nodded, her brown eyes wide and bewildered as she docilely let him lead her across the room. Just when she thought she was beginning to understand Santine, he did something to prove that she had scarcely scratched the surface. She had expected him to be his usual autocratic self this evening, judging from those last curt sentences on the terrace. Yet she was sure she'd detected an undercurrent of gentleness, perhaps even tenderness, in his voice.

"You must be very quick," Santine was murmuring in her ear as they slowly traversed the length of the room. "When I saw you playing in the fountain an hour ago, I really didn't think you'd make it down on time."

She cast him a startled glance. "You saw me at the fountain?" she asked.

"I was in the library," he said softly. "After Stokley told me you weren't in your room, I assumed you'd gone back to the gazebo, and I was watching for you at the window." His lips curved in a little smile. "I was a trifle vexed with you, to put it mildly. Then you came dancing into the courtyard barefoot and tousled as a happy child and decided to play in the fountain. It was a rather enchanting sight." His dark gaze narrowed curiously on her surprised face. "Tell me, why were you staring so disapprovingly at my bell tower?"

"Oh, it wasn't disapproval. I like it very much," she assured him absently, still feeling a trifle dazed by the knowledge that those wild, foolish moments had been observed by Santine. "It was just that I'd forgotten those shutters when I built my sand castle."

"Sand castle?" he said blankly, then he suddenly threw back his head and laughed aloud. Several guests stopped their casual chatter to gaze at him in discreet amazement, but he ignored them with typical arrogance. "You were building sand castles on the beach all afternoon?"

"Not all afternoon," she said dreamily. "Part of the time I was walking on the beach and playing in the surf. I had a wonderful time."

"I can see that you did," he said, his gaze on her glowing face, and there was again that odd gentleness in their darkness. "I wish that I could have been there to watch you." They had reached the small cluster of guests that had been Santine's objective, and he pulled his gaze from her with obvious reluctance. Then, as if by magic, that bewildering gentleness was gone, replaced by his usual mockery as he smoothly performed the introductions.

There were only five people in the small group in the corner, but from the careless attentiveness of Santine's demeanor she guessed they were the primary players in Santine's game that evening. The only one she had met previously was Pat Dawson, who was looking surprisingly sophisticated in his tuxedo. He acknowledged her murmured greeting with a warm smile and a glint of admiration in his eyes.

The other members of the group were two couples Santine introduced as Harry and Sylvia Waterman and James and Elizabeth Sanders. All four were apparently in their early fifties, with the sleek, expensive patina that the rest of the assemblage possessed. She immediately recognized Sylvia Waterman's high, shrill voice as the one that had made her cringe when she'd entered the room, and the woman's shallow, flighty conversation matched her piercing voice precisely.

They were all carefully courteous to her as she stood there under the subtle cloak of protection that Santine draped about her, but she was much relieved when he nodded imperiously to Dawson and said smoothly, "Pat, why don't you take Janna to the bar and get her a drink? We don't want to bore her with our dull business affairs." He smiled charmingly at the other women in the group. "I'd tell you to escort these other lovely ladies, too, but I may need them to use their charms on their husbands in my behalf."

"Delighted," Dawson said promptly, coming forward eagerly to take Janna's arm. "That's the best offer I've had all evening. Come along, Miss Cannon; let's see how many drinks I can ply you with before dinner. I always look better to women through an alcoholic haze."

"One drink," Santine ordered tersely. "Miss Cannon didn't eat any lunch." He turned back to his business associates with that charming, sociable smile Janna found so incongruous with what she now knew of his character.

There was a quizzical grin on Dawson's face as he propelled her in the general direction of the bar. "It seems I made a slight error in judgment," he murmured. "That look Mr. Santine gave me nearly took the top of my head off." He darted her a speculative glance. "How the hell did you manage to rouse the protective instinct in my employer's savage breast? I've never seen him display that particular emotion for anyone before."

Janna shook her head ruefully. "I'm afraid you're mistaken," she said dryly. "I scarcely know the man, and I'm quite sure protectiveness isn't a quality he'd feel toward me if I'd known him for a decade."

"I admit that it's unusual," he drawled. "But then, so is giving a two-million-dollar land grant to a pretty trespasser he'd never seen before." He raised an inquiring eyebrow. "You wouldn't like to enlighten me as to what went on in the library after Santine sent me away, would you?"

She shook her head firmly.

"I didn't think so." He sighed resignedly. "It appears that my curiosity is going to go unsatisfied. I understand we're going to have the pleasure of your company for a time."

"For a time," she replied reservedly, and heard Dawson's amused chuckle.

"Okay, I can take a hint," he said lightly, his blue eyes twinkling. "I'll concede that discussion of anything pertaining to your rather bizarre arrival last night is taboo. I'll expect a return favor of you, however."

"Favor?" she asked warily, her eyes on his face.

He nodded with a grimace. "I'm not looking forward to being marooned down here for two months with only Santine for companionship. I was hoping you'd take pity on my solitary state occasionally. Purely platonic, of course. I'm not about to step on Santine's toes, whatever your relationship with him."

She studied him soberly and then smiled warmly into his wholesome, friendly face. "I'd like that," she said softly. "I have a feeling I may need a friend myself in the coming weeks."

"Good," Dawson said briskly. "Now, what can I get you to drink to fill that meager ration Santine has allowed you?"

"Just some tomato juice," Janna said quietly. "I don't drink."

Dawson gave her a surprised glance before he shrugged. "Whatever you say," he said casually. "I'll be right back."

True to his word, he was swiftly back at her side, with a frosty goblet containing the innocuous beverage, which he handed her with a flourish. Taking a swallow of his own whiskey and looking across the room at the little coterie surrounding Santine, he observed idly, "It looks like the boss is operating on all cylinders tonight. I'll wager he'll have Waterman eating out of his hand by the end of the evening."

"Why should he want to do that?" Janna asked curiously, sipping her tomato juice slowly. "I thought Mr. Santine could pretty well call the shots in any business transaction he entered into."

"He can," Dawson agreed coolly. "But forcible take-overs can be expensive, and he wants Silverline Computers rather badly. If he can persuade Waterman and Sanders to vote their sizable blocks of stock in his favor, the take-over will be almost bloodless."

"And if not?" Janna asked slowly, her eyes on Santine's enigmatic face as he listened attentively to something Sanders was explaining.

"Then he'll get it anyway," Dawson said casually. "It will just take longer." His lips curled sardonically. "And I guarantee that it won't be bloodless if they force him to go to the extra trouble."

At that moment Stokley appeared at the arched doorway and announced with regal dignity that dinner was served. Dawson offered Janna his arm with a mocking panache. "My lady," he drawled gallantly. "I assume I'm to take you in to dinner, since Santine hasn't reclaimed you."

She smiled as she slipped her arm through his, and they drifted slowly toward the door. As they passed the expressionless Stokley still standing at military attention, she obeyed a sudden impulse and gave him a conspiratorial wink. "I made it, Stokley," she murmured in an undertone as she passed him on Dawson's arm.

"I see that you did, Miss Cannon," he replied softly, his lips barely moving. "May I say that you also look charming?"

"You may," she said impishly, raising her head regally. She heard a queer choked sound emit from Stokley's throat as she passed out of earshot.

Dawson was looking at her, his brow creased in perplexity. "What was that all about?" he demanded as they passed into the dining room at the far end of the foyer.

"Nothing," Janna answered demurely, a tiny smile hovering on her lips. "Nothing at all."

The rest of the evening wasn't nearly as tedious as she'd feared, thanks to Pat Dawson's good-humored charm and assiduous attentions. He kept her constantly laughing at his wry, slightly acerbic comments on their fellow guests both during dinner and later, when they were served coffee in the living room. The evening passed with such amazing swiftness that, in what seemed a short time later, Janna was astonished to see Santine bidding farewell to a number of guests.

Dawson also noticed the flurry and stood up with obvious reluctance, holding his hand out to pull Janna to her feet. "I think we'd better wander over and do our social duty," he said with a grimace. "I see Waterman and Sanders are about ready to leave. As I did the preliminary groundwork on the merger, I'll be expected to keep up a cordial facade until we have their proxies. I think I may catch hell from Santine anyway, for neglecting them. I noticed he was casting some distinctly icy glances at us this evening."

Janna frowned in puzzlement. "Are you sure?" she asked. "He always seemed to be very much involved whenever I saw him tonight."

"I'm sure," he said wryly. "I've made quite a study of Rafe Santine's temperament over the years, and I assure you that he wasn't pleased with me." They had reached the perimeter of the group at the door now, and Pat painted a bright, cordial smile on his face that looked surprisingly sincere.

Stokley and two of the maids were busy fetching the coats and evening wraps from the guest closets in the foyer, and she exchanged a faint smile with Stokley before Dawson placed a hand on her arm and nudged her gently to where Santine was standing, conversing with the Watermans and the Sanders. Santine looked up as they approached, and Janna knew immediately that Pat was right. Something had put him in a ferocious temper.

"Janna, my dear," he greeted her silkily, reaching out to pluck her from Dawson's hold, his arm sliding around her waist in swift possession. "We thought you'd forgotten us in your absorption with my fascinating assistant, here." His hand tightened almost painfully on her slim waist. "Now you only have time to say good night to our guests."

Our guests? Janna darted him an incredulous glance. He was behaving as if she were a hostess who had been derelict in her duties, when only this morning he'd assured her she need not even talk to his precious dinner guests if she didn't choose to do so. The man changed the rules from moment to moment.

She turned to Harry Waterman, who was closest to her, and offered her hand. "It was a pleasure meeting you, Mr. Waterman," she said quietly. "I hope that I see you again soon."

The small rotund man pumped her hand heartily, his fleshy jowls trembling. "I'm sure you will, Miss Cannon," he beamed. "Rafe, here, tells me you're going to be staying on to finalize the details on some charity project he's interested in. We're bound to run into each other in the next few weeks."

So Pat had been right, Janna thought. Waterman had obviously been persuaded to go along with Santine's cause in the course of the evening. She withdrew her hand and was about to turn to Sanders when she heard Dawson give a low whistle. "Great heavens, that's a gorgeous coat, Sylvia," he said admiringly. "It's absolutely stunning against the darkness of your hair."

Janna glanced automatically in Sylvia Waterman's direction, and her breath caught in her throat. The soft, lustrous full-length fur coat did flatter the woman's elaborately coiffed black hair, she thought numbly. The black stripes on the orange-gold background were almost the exactly same shade.

"Do you really think so, Pat?" Sylvia Waterman gushed as she put her arms in the fur coat, which Stokley was holding, and shrugged into it. "I've wanted a tiger-skin coat for simply ages, but it's extremely hard to get hold of a really nice one." Her hand ran caressingly along the silky fur of the front lapels, her long, beautifully manicured nails bright red against the golden pelt. Blood red. "It's so much more unique than mink or sable, don't you think?" She tucked one arm in her husband's and fluttered her eyelashes coyly at him. "Harry bought it for me in India last year, when we were on our round-the-world tour. It's really the only decent place to obtain decent tiger skins these days. It took Harry almost a week to locate someone who could get the quantity of skins needed for a full-length coat." She squeezed his arm affectionately. "But when Harry wants something, there's no standing in his way."

Waterman nodded with smug satisfaction. "You've just got to have the contacts and pay the price."

Janna felt as if she were going to be sick. Her entire body was cold and clammy, as if it were encased in ice. She couldn't take her eyes from Sylvia Waterman's hand that was still clutching the fur. Such a dainty hand to be so horribly, selfishly greedy. "Where did you get it?" she choked hoarsely, her throat dry and tight. "Where did you get the skins?"

Sylvia Waterman's pale blue eyes widened in surprise as she glanced over at Janna. "Why, I told you, dear," she said patiently. "Harry bought it for me in India. Where did that funny little man have to send to get the furs, Harry?"

"Nepal," he replied casually, patting her hand absently. "And we had to wait damn near two weeks to get them. Those Indians have no sense of the value of time."

"Nepal," Janna repeated faintly, and she could feel the waves of nausea wash through her. "Nepal."

"Are you all right, Janna?" Santine asked, frowning, his eyes on her dazed face. "You're as white as a sheet."

From far away she could see them all staring at her with varying degrees of puzzlement, as if from the opposite end of a tunnel. "Please excuse me," she muttered numbly. "I'm not feeling very well." Then she was hurrying away from them, her mind blank, only her instincts carrying her toward the courtyard door.

"Janna!"

She heard Santine's imperious shout, but it failed to pierce the ice that was wrapping her in its comforting embrace. She was in the courtyard, running across it, the cool, crisp autumn air striking sharply against her hot cheeks. Strange they should be hot, when the rest of her felt so cold.

Then she was in the woods, running blindly through the shrubbery. She could feel the branches and bushes tearing at her as she raced mindlessly through the estate grounds. She had no idea of destination, yet she wasn't really surprised when she broke free of the woods and found herself on the top of the cliff. The outline of the gazebo was a graceful welcoming sight against the star-flung darkness of the horizon. It looked oddly comforting, almost homelike, to Janna in that moment of desolation, and she crept within its shelter like a wounded animal seeking a cave to lick its wounds.

Four

Janna curled on the cushioned gazebo seat, tucking her feet beneath her and leaning on the redwood railing, while she stared sightlessly into the moonlit darkness. The ice was beginning to melt now, as she'd feared it would, and the pain was a throbbing ache in her breast. She could feel the silent tears running helplessly down her cheeks, but she made no attempt to stop them. Someone should cry, damn it. Someone should care.

"I thought I'd find you here," Santine said grimly, from the entrance of the gazebo. Though the black-and-white elegance of his tuxedo appeared as immaculate as ever, his hair was ruffled and he was breathing heavily, as if he'd been running. "Now, will you kindly explain what the hell that was all about back there?"

She didn't answer as he came slowly forward and sat down beside her. She could feel his eyes on her in the shadowed dimness of the redwood canopy, but for the first time since she'd met him, she was not experiencing that suffocating electric awareness. He was just a presence in the darkness.

"Did you notice how red her fingernails were?" she asked numbly, not looking at him. Somehow those blood-red-tipped claws buried so sensuously in the fur wouldn't leave her mind.

"Sylvia Waterman's?" Santine asked impatiently. She could see his shadowed face frown in puzzlement.

"You'll forgive me if I can't comprehend what Sylvia's rather garish manicure has to do with this."

"Tiger, tiger, burning bright, in the forest of the night," Janna quoted feverishly, the tears flowing faster now, her throat aching. "So beautiful. But there won't be any more tigers in the forest, will there?"

"Is that why you're so upset?" Santine asked, frowning. "Because Sylvia Waterman had the bad taste to buy a tiger-skin coat?"

"Do you know how many tigers had to die to create a coat of that quality?" Janna asked huskily. "To match those stripes so exactly?" Her voice broke. "Do you know how many tigers are left in the world?"

"My God, you're crying," Santine said wonderingly. He reached out a hand to tilt her face up, so that the dappled moonlight fell on her brimming eyes and tear-streaked cheeks. "Oh, hell!" Janna felt herself being pulled forcefully into his embrace, her face crushed into the starched crispness of his white shirt. She could feel the strong beat of his heart beneath her ear and the deep, ragged breaths he took. His tone was a curious blend of exasperation and helplessness as he repeated, "Oh, hell!"

Janna's arms automatically encircled him as she burrowed her head deeper in his chest, conscious only of the warm comfort of his hard male strength. "And they came from Nepal," she sobbed bitterly. "No wonder it took so long to get them. They have the largest Bengal tiger reserve in the world in Nepal. The poachers would have to be very careful in order to bag that many cats without being caught." She rubbed her wet cheeks against his shirt, not caring that the cloth was damp with her tears. "But Harry Waterman made it worth their while, didn't he? I wonder how many crowns *he* would have given for a great auk?"

"I wish you'd quit crying," Santine said huskily. His large hands, moving gently on her slim back,

were strangely awkward. "God, I can't stand this."
One hand moved up to massage the tense muscles
of her nape. "And what the hell is a great auk?"

"Nothing any more," she said brokenly, almost to
herself. "They were gentle, dignified birds that looked
a little like penguins. Their skin became tremendously sought after by European collectors, and by
the early eighteen hundreds millions of them had
been slaughtered. Finally all the great auks left on
earth were on the island of Elderly, in Scandinavia.
But they couldn't leave them alone even then. An
agent for the European buyers offered fifty crowns
each for their skins, and an Icelandic fisherman
took a crew to Elderly to make his fortune." Her lips
curved bitterly. "He searched thoroughly but he found
only two great auks on the entire island. He killed
them and took their skins back to Reykjavik to col-
lect his reward. He didn't care that he'd just killed
the last two great auks left on the face of the earth."
She drew a deep, shuddering breath. "And now there
are hundreds of species that are on the point of
extinction and they still don't care. No one really
cares if all that wonder and beauty disappears from
our world."

"You care," Santine said hoarsely, his lips buried
in the soft hair at her temple. "My God, but you
care!" One hand moved to close around the thick silki-
ness of her braid. "I'm not equipped to handle this
kind of thing, damn it. Didn't anyone ever tell you that
Indians are supposed to be stoic?"

"Did I tell you that we had two baby cheetahs born
at our own reserve this year?" she murmured softly.
The silent tears were falling in a seemingly endless
stream. "We were over the moon with joy. Cheetahs
refuse to reproduce in captivity, you know."

"No, I didn't know," he growled, with a note of
desperation in his deep, gravelly voice. "But I do
know that I can't stand much more of this. What the

hell can I give you to make you stop this infernal crying?"

"Give me?" Janna asked vaguely, lifting her head to look up at him in bewilderment. Her wide-set brown eyes were glistening mistily in the moonlight, and her thin, tear-streaked face appeared heart-shakingly poignant to the man gazing down at it. "I don't understand. What do you mean?"

Santine gave a rough impatient imprecation and pulled her face back into his shirtfront. "For God's sake, don't look at me like that! It wasn't supposed to be like this, damn it. I've never felt like this in my life. What the hell are you trying to do to me?" There was outrage mixed with an odd note of pain in his voice, and he drew a long shaky breath. "Do you want me to break Waterman so that he can't ever indulge that stupid bitch of a wife again? Would that help?"

"What?" This time she pushed herself entirely out of his arms, to gaze up at him incredulously. "You can't mean that."

His lips curved in a grim smile. "Try me," he said tersely, his powerful hands holding her shoulders as if they were delicate as eggshells, and looking down at her with an intensity that caused her to tremble slightly in his grasp. "I don't give a damn about Waterman one way or the other. If it would make you happier, I'll put the skids under him without a qualm. Shall I do it?"

She shook her head dazedly. "No, of course not," she said huskily. "That would make me as much of a destroyer as they are." She bit her lower lip in perplexity. "But why would you do that for me?"

"How the hell should I know?" he muttered in exasperation, giving her shoulders a little shake. "I think I've gone a little crazy since the moment I saw you last night. Why should I care that you're so soft that you bleed inside at the sight of a blasted fur coat? Why should I feel your pain as if it were my own? It doesn't make any sense, damn it. I don't want to feel like this toward *anyone*, much less some little starry-eyed idealist who has no more defenses than a day-old kitten."

Her eyes were wide and startled looking at his hard stormy face, and she instinctively made a motion to move away from him. It was a move that was frustrated immediately by the possessive tightening of his hands on her shoulders. "No, stay where you are," he said thickly. "I won't hurt you, little doe. I don't think I've ever known tenderness for a woman before. It feels strange as hell. Come here, Janna."

He drew her carefully into his arms, and she flowed wearily into them with a strange sense of inevitability. His hands were gently massaging her back in an almost hypnotically soothing motion, all of his former awkwardness gone. "You look so fragile," he said, "yet I can feel the warmth and strength of you under my hands." Those hands were exploring the lithe tendons in the small of her back with the curiosity a child might show, yet they generated a slow-building heat that caused her to melt closer to him with a little indrawn breath.

He flinched as if the touch of her had burned him, and she could feel his muscles tense and harden against her yielding softness. "Mine," he muttered softly, his arms tightening around her. "Why do you feel as if you belong to me? I thought I just wanted to comfort you, but all I had to do was brush against you and you've got me ready to tear your clothes off and lose myself in that smooth, supple body." His hands traveled slowly from the small of her back to the soft yellow jersey that covered one shoulder, and bared it with a deliberation that caused Janna to rouse momentarily from her state of languid apathy and try to wriggle away from him.

"No," she whispered frantically, her hands pushing lightly against his chest. "I don't belong to you. I don't belong to anyone. Let me go."

"Shhhh," he said tenderly as his lips brushed gently against the soft, vulnerable skin beneath her collarbone. She could feel the flesh tauten and burn beneath the teasing touch of his tongue. "Can't you see that I can't let you go? I don't like what's happened, but it's too late to worry about that now for either of us. I think it was too late the first time I saw you walking across the courtyard."

"You weren't even sure that I appealed to you last night," she protested faintly, while his lips moved toward the hollow of her throat, lingering on the pulse that was beating so erratically.

"You appealed to me all right," he growled softly, his lips traveling up the graceful cord of her neck to her ear and nibbling gently at her earlobe. "I watched you sitting there before me on the ottoman with those big brown eyes gazing at me like an earnest child, and all I could think of was how much I'd like to see you lying naked in my bed holding out your arms to me and pleading with me to love you. I'd never wanted anyone so much before in my life."

Janna's breath caught in her throat, and she was beginning to feel an odd aching in her loins. Every word muttered in that sandpaper-velvet voice was escalating the molten heat that seemed to be flowing in every vein of her body. "Yet you didn't take me," she said huskily, her head swimming dizzily.

"You scared the hell out of me," he said incredibly, his lips hovering only a breath away from her own. "I wasn't about to be dragged into an obsessive relationship that I couldn't control. I had to reject you to prove that I could do it." His tongue was gently tracing the line of her lower lip. "Open your mouth, Janna. I've got to know the taste of you."

She parted her lips, and his eager tongue entered to explore and slake himself on her inner sweetness, his hands rhythmically kneading the muscles of her back while his lips drank thirstily from the bounty that she offered. She heard him utter a deep, animal groan somewhere deep in his throat, and she could feel his muscles tauten with an almost unbearable tension.

With one swift movement, without even breaking the contact of their lips, he scooped her up and transferred her to his lap, where he cradled her in his arms. She was dazedly conscious, through the thin jersey of her gown, of his hard arousal, and she felt a little frisson of fear run through her. She was suddenly aware of how small and fragile she was in comparison to his virile maleness. He was all massive muscle and aggressive drive. If he chose, he could break the delicate femininity in his grasp with effortless ease. Then, incredibly, she felt that massive body tremble, and she knew it was need for her that had shaken him. Her own fear suddenly vanished in the wake of the surge of joyous power that flowed through her.

His lips left hers, and he buried his head against her throat, his breathing hard and shallow. "God, I want you," he said thickly. "I was jealous as a schoolboy tonight when I watched you laughing and talking with Dawson. I didn't want you smiling at anyone like that except me."

"But you sent me away with him," she protested faintly as he pushed the yellow gown totally off her shoulder and nibbled gently at the smooth skin of her upper arm.

His teeth suddenly nipped sharply at her soft flesh. "You weren't supposed to enjoy it so much," he said tersely. "Next time, you're not going to be more than a foot away from me all evening." His hands moved around to her back, and suddenly she felt a cool waft of air as he deftly slid down the zipper. She inhaled sharply when she felt his large warm hands on her naked back, and she stiffened involuntarily in his arms.

"Easy, love," he murmured softly, and his voice was amazingly tender, completely lacking its usual brisk abrasiveness. "I'm not going to hurt you. You're such a sweet, wild thing." His hands were moving soothingly on her back, gentling her as if she were the wild thing he had called her. "I just want to fill my hands with you. You feel like golden silk beneath my fingers." His hands moved around and were suddenly cupping the fullness of her breasts in his palms. "God, what a lovely, sweet weight they are," he said hoarsely, his lips pressing tiny hot kisses on her throat and cheeks. "I want to see them."

His lips covered hers in a hot, liquid kiss, while his hands slowly nudged the bodice of her gown to her waist and then were once more on the peaked thrust of her breasts, his thumbs teasing the nipples into burgeoning hardness. Janna felt her breasts swell and harden beneath that sensuous touch as if they were offering themselves at his demand. She made a tiny little sound that was half plea, half moan, but it was lost beneath the urgency of his lips on hers. Then he was releasing her and pushing her gently away, his eyes narrowed on her breasts with an intensity that was as scorching as the teasing manipulation of his hands. One finger delicately traced the dusky pink nipple.

"Beautiful," he breathed huskily, his hand lifting the firm mounds in his hands. "All lovely shades of cream and tan and pink. You're what the primitive tribes must have envisioned as the perfect earth mother."

His head slowly lowered as if driven inexorably, and his lips brushed a taut nipple in a delicate caress that caused a shudder of sheer, primitive need to run through her. His tongue joined his teasing lips in the gentle salutes to each breast before he glanced up at her, his dark eyes holding hers with mesmerizing intimacy. "Bring me to your lovely breasts and let me suckle, little earth mother," he said thickly, and almost without thinking Janna's hands reached up to curl in the heavy darkness of his hair and pulled his lips to her breasts.

He gave a feverish moan of satisfaction as his lips closed on her engorged nipple and suckled at it with tongue, teeth, and the strong suction of his lips. It was an incredibly arousing caress, and with each tantalizing tug she felt a jolt of heat shoot through every limb. His mouth moved over to the other breast and began the same ritual of burning caresses. By this time Janna could only clutch his silky dark head to her in a bewildering daze of heat and aching need, her breath coming in little gasps and her eyes closed against the wave of desire that was running through her like a rioting river.

"Open your eyes, Janna," Santine demanded hoarsely, raising his head. "I want to know that you're wanting me as much as I want you."

Her lids fluttered open with almost drugged languor, and she gazed up at him, her brown eyes clouded with emotion. She was vaguely aware that his eyes were fastened on her with an urgent demand in their depths, but she was too bewildered, too lost in the haze of desire he'd woven about her, to comprehend what it was he wanted of her.

"Janna, I'm in a fever for you," he said thickly. "Will you come to my bed and let me love you tonight?"

The stilted phrasing sounded oddly formal on Santine's lips, she thought dreamily. But why was he asking her such a ridiculous question, when he must realize she wanted nothing more than the fiery completion that he'd been building toward? Besides, hadn't something been said about that last night? she thought hazily. She frowned and tried to concentrate, but the languid tightening in her loins was mounting steadily, and she suddenly didn't want to think. She only wanted him to stop gazing at her with that fierce frown and take her back in his arms. But it appeared he wasn't going to do it unless she answered that absurd question.

Her brow wrinkled in an impatient frown as she said huskily, "Yes, of course. I told you last night that I would." She waited expectantly for him to draw her back in his embrace.

But his reaction wasn't what she had anticipated. Instead of the renewed blaze of desire, his dark eyes widened with a curious look of shock. Then they flared with a smoldering anger that caught Janna completely by surprise. Her eyes widened as his expression hardened before darkening stormily. "That's right, you did," he said coldly as he scooped her off his lap onto the cushioned bench beside him. "I'm afraid I'd forgotten how readily you agreed to my terms." His lips twisted bitterly. "What did you call it? Oh yes, a 'simple biological coupling.'"

Janna gazed at him bewilderedly as he smoothed his hair and got jerkily to his feet. One moment she'd been involved in the most passionate experience of her entire life and the next she'd been shunted away from Santine as if she had the plague. Distractedly she reached up to brush a stray lock of hair behind her ear, and moistened her lips nervously. "What happened?" she faltered huskily, looking up at him dazedly. "Don't you want me any more?"

"You're damn right I want you," Santine said with soft violence, leaning down and jerking her gown up to cover her naked breasts. "I'm tempted to spread these cushions on the floor and take you right here and now." He put her left arm through the single strap of the gown as impersonally as if he were dressing a small child, pulling the jersey over her shoulder before swiftly zipping the back. "But I'm not going to let you gain that kind of power over me until I can be sure I mean more to you than the payoff of a debt." He straightened slowly and looked down at her with narrowed eyes. "I've discovered that you're a very dangerous lady as far as I'm concerned, Janna. You're fast becoming something of an obsession, and I'm not at all pleased with the situation. I've become accustomed to being totally in control of my life and emotions. I won't be put into a position where either one can be manipulated."

Janna experienced a queer thrust of pain that pierced the sensual mist that had enveloped her. What had she been thinking of, to be so beguiled by the sexual expertise of a man like Santine? That he considered her dangerous was almost laughable when viewed in the light of his threat to her. As he had said, Santine liked to be in complete control, and she'd already discovered how possessive he could be. He would never tolerate the personal freedom that was essential to her even if he came to care for her. And that possibility was probably very slim indeed, she thought wryly. She'd been offered lust, not love, tonight.

She sat up straight and looked up at him steadily. "Then wouldn't it be wiser to send me away?" she asked coolly. "That would solve all your problems."

"Would it?" Santine's lips twisted. "Somehow I don't think so. I have an idea that I'd last about a day before I sent someone to bring you back to me." His hand reached out, as if compulsively, to touch her thick, lustrous braid. "Like I said, it's an obsession." He pulled his hand away reluctantly and drew a deep breath. "No, you'll stay with me until I can rid myself of it. They say that nearness breeds boredom, and it always has before for me." He smiled mockingly. "You'll be my little pet, whom I can stroke or ignore at will. And when I've regained my perspective enough to take you to bed without its meaning a thing, I'm going to make love to that gorgeous body in every way I can think of."

He turned and strode swiftly out of the gazebo and down the path toward the woods beyond.

• • •

In the next week it seemed Santine was determined to treat Janna as the pet he had termed her. He insisted that she not only eat all her meals with him, but that she be his constant companion no matter what activity he was engaged in. Janna found herself playing chess, going for long sunrise swims, and listening to records on Santine's magnificent stereo system. Even when he was involved in business with Dawson or one of the vice presidents who flew in for an occasional meeting when urgency demanded, she was ordered to be present. This usually meant that she sat quietly curled up in Santine's brown leather chair with a book she seldom bothered even to pretend to read.

Santine in action was much more fascinating to study than the most interesting printed word. He was brisk, dynamic, and totally brilliant. In addition, he had a driving energy that was almost boundless, and an incisiveness that cut unerringly to the marrow of any subject he was confronted with. If this was Rafe Santine at leisure, she wondered ruefully what he must be like when he was operating at full strength. Even when he was occupied with supposed leisure pursuits, he exhibited a restlessness and competitiveness Janna found simply astounding. She had a shrewd idea that more than big business was a game to Rafe Santine. Every facet of his life seemed to fall into that category, and he played it with keen gusto.

She gradually discovered there were other, more human characteristics to admire in Santine than the drive and the brilliance that had made him a legend. He possessed a wry sense of humor that surfaced unexpectedly from time to time to surprise and delight her, and, though cynical to the extreme, he never let his natural skepticism interfere with his innate sense of justice. She supposed the aspect of his personality she found most attractive was the insatiable thirst for knowledge that was almost a passion with him. He had a curiosity that was easily aroused and, once stirred, would not be satisfied until he'd plumbed the depth of the subject that had intrigued him. Janna soon found he was far better informed on art and politics than she, and he was practically an authority on medieval history, which he found completely fascinating.

Santine was almost entirely self-educated, having left school at sixteen to go to work on his first construction job. It was all the more praiseworthy that beneath the deliberately rough facade he presented, he was possibly the most cultured individual Janna had ever known.

It was strange that two such contrasting personalities should be able to develop the curious companionship that had evolved between them in the last week. Santine seemed to find Janna's serenity and lack of aggressiveness oddly soothing, while his restless energy had an exhilarating effect on her usually quiet nature. If it weren't for the subtle sexual tension pervading their relationship, Janna felt they might even have become friends.

But that the tension did exist was undeniable. Santine seemed to view her with a wariness that increased rather than diminished with association. He avoided touching her with scrupulous care, and she was equally cautious. She wanted no more of Santine's soul-scorching lovemaking if she could avoid it. It was far too dangerous for her to trifle with. She had the uneasy sensation that a tiny portion of her had flowed into Santine that night at the gazebo and would never be returned to her. She wouldn't chance any more loss of the essence that comprised her own personality and independence.

She knew now she hadn't underestimated Santine's possessiveness. Though he'd made no move to claim the sexual privileges he had bargained for, he made quite sure it was known that he considered her his exclusive property. Even Dawson and Stokley weren't exempted from his jealous surveillance when he chanced to come upon her laughing and joking with them. Both men were made to feel Santine's immediate displeasure, and he made every effort to be sure she wasn't allowed to repeat the casual encounters.

Even when he was offered no **overt** provocation there were moments when he **would** gaze at her with a smoldering possessiveness that filled her with a panicky feeling of claustrophobia. It was during these times that he would probe silkily at her with intimate questions that caused her to grit her teeth to prevent her from saying the words which would jeopardize the fragile balance of their relationship. She tried to answer his moody insinuations with evasive politeness, but she found it increasingly difficult to maintain her coolness. He seemed to believe that she'd been sexually promiscuous since her infancy, she thought in exasperation, and the questions regarding the men in her past bordered on being downright ridiculous. She would have to be a nymphomaniac to have bedded all the men he suspected her of entertaining. Even if she'd possessed the experience he attributed to her, it was entirely her own business, and she wasn't about to satisfy his curiosity. She was aware that her reticence infuriated Santine and only served to aggravate his suspicions, but she stubbornly stuck to her resolve to maintain her privacy.

In less than two months she would be out of Santine's life, perhaps never to see him again. It would be foolish to let him think she would docilely accept his prying. It was not as if he were anything of a celibate himself, she thought defensively. Diane Simmons was still very much in evidence at the castle. She seemed to accept Janna's presence at Santine's side with perfect tranquility, and he continued to treat her with a slightly impatient tolerance that

Janna found oddly comforting. Not that she fooled herself that Santine's rejection of the gorgeous blonde extended to the bedroom. Diane Simmons was just a little too complacent to be a woman entirely scorned. Well, why should that bother her? If Diane was fulfilling his sexual needs, surely this made her own position safer. That was what she wanted, wasn't it?

Santine's moodiness increased as the week wore on, along with his bad temper, and by the end of the day Janna wanted nothing more than to escape from those brooding, dark eyes and the razor-sharp tongue. Tonight his sarcasm was so blatant it had pierced even Diane's cheerful blindness, and she had discreetly withdrawn to her room immediately after dinner. Pat Dawson was not so lucky, and had to accept the blistering edge of his censure of a transaction that he'd presumably bungled. It was only when Santine was forced to answer an urgent phone call from one of his overseas subsidiaries that Dawson was let off the hook.

He breathed a profound sigh of relief, his eyes fixed warily on Santine at the desk across the room before turning to Janna. "Saved by the bell," he murmured. "I thought he was going to fire me, for a minute, there."

"Was it such a grave mistake?" Janna asked gently, her eyes on his slightly flushed face. She had come to like Pat Dawson very much in the last week. His light, dry humor had been a pleasant relief from Rafe Santine's smoldering moodiness.

Dawson shrugged. "I've made worse," he said with a grimace. "But not when he was in such a foul humor. He's been practically savage for days now." His eyebrows raised mockingly. "I don't have to tell you that. As much time as you're spending with him, you're probably getting more than your share."

"Yes," Janna said absently, her gaze following Dawson's to the figure at the desk. Santine was dressed in black slacks and a sportcoat that contrasted strikingly with his scarlet turtleneck sweater. His hair was slightly rumpled, and one lock was lying on his forehead, giving him a careless, slightly piratical look. Evidently what he was hearing wasn't pleasing him, for his frown was darkening more by the second. "He's not been easy to live with lately."

Pat's eyes narrowed speculatively on her face. "I imagine a great deal of the blame can be laid at your door, pretty lady," he said quietly, leaning forward to pick up his coffee cup from the end table between them. "You seem to have a very turbulent effect on my employer. If you weren't such charming company, I'd wish you a thousand miles away from here. It would increase my job security enormously."

Janna's eyes widened in surprise. Pat must really have been having a difficult time, to make such a remark. "I'm sorry you're having problems," she said, smiling at him. "I don't think I'll be here much longer. As you say, I seem to have a very irritating effect on Rafe."

"I wouldn't be too sure of that," he said thoughtfully, taking a sip of his coffee and regarding her gravely over the rim. "I've never seen him act like this about a woman before. I'm half afraid even to talk to you."

Janna's lashes swept down to veil her eyes. "I'm sure I'm not the sole cause for his displeasure," she said quietly. "He wasn't exactly a model of charm and sweetness when I appeared on the scene."

"True," Pat conceded ruefully. "This forced sabbatical is playing hell with his nerves, but he certainly didn't look upon my humble self as a threat before." His lips curved wryly. "I can't say that I'm relishing the position. Threats to Rafe Santine have a tendency to be smashed underfoot."

She lifted her eyes to regard him gravely. "Yet you've been with him for a long time."

"I respect him," he said laconically. "He's something of a phenomenon, and he doesn't begrudge his employees their own share of the pie if they have the initiative to go after it." He grinned. "Besides, he's more fun than a barrel of monkeys to watch when he moves into high gear. I've learned more from him in two years than I would with any other businessman in fifty. That doesn't preclude my being very healthily intimidated by the man."

"Respect, admiration, and fear," she murmured softly, her eyes sad. "Such cold emotions for a man to inspire in the people around him."

Dawson's lips curved cynically. "Don't waste your sympathy. Those are the only emotions Santine wants to inspire. He doesn't have any use for the softer feelings." He stretched out his legs lazily in front of him, his eyes fixed thoughtfully on the polished black tips of his shoes. "Not that you can blame him for a certain lack of trust in his fellow man, when you consider his background. Did you know he was illegitimate?"

Janna nodded slowly. "It's fairly common knowledge. The newspapers love the poor-boy-makes-good-against-all-odds bit."

"He has no idea who his father is, and his mother was little better than a prostitute. She deserted him when he was eight, and he lived with a series of foster parents, who apparently cared more for the welfare money than for an orphaned kid. They evidently let him run pretty wild. It's a wonder that he didn't end up in a reform school."

It was indeed, Janna mused, feeling a queer little tug at her heartstrings. It was amazing he'd survived with as few emotional scars as he had. How could she condemn him for believing that every woman had the instincts of an alley cat, when he'd probably known nothing else since the moment of his conception? She could feel a suspicious moistness mist her eyes, and her throat tightened painfully. The wave of sympathy brought with it an element of sheer panic. No, she mustn't feel this melting tenderness at the thought of that troubled, vulnerable little boy. Pat was right. Rafe was hard as a stone, and had no use for love and tenderness. Love? My God, what must she be thinking of? She couldn't love Rafe Santine. She wouldn't love him. It was only pity that stirred her heart in this odd fashion.

She jumped to her feet and put her cup and saucer hurriedly on the coffee table. Dawson looked up inquiringly at her sudden action. "I've got to make a telephone call," she said quickly, moistening her dry lips and trying to hide the urgent need to escape from Santine's presence that she was experiencing. "This is the evening I have to call my grandmother."

Dawson glanced at his employer at the massive desk. "It looks like he might be talking to Paris for quite some time."

"I'll use the extension in the hall," she said, moving swiftly toward the door. "I'd rather not wait. My grandmother goes to bed early these days."

Santine looked up and frowned absently as she slipped through the door and closed it softly behind her.

She moved swiftly through the foyer to the elegant telephone table by the curve of the staircase and sank down on the cushioned bench. A few minutes later the connection was made, and she recognized the deep, masculine tones of Jody Forrester, the manager of her grandmother's farm.

"Jody?" Her voice was anxious despite the effort she was making to steady it. "This is Janna. How is she?"

Jody's voice was gentle and soothing. "She's doing fine, Janna. She went for a long walk today up to your hill and stayed there most of the afternoon. When she came back, she was tired but very contented. She told me that you are always with her there, Janna."

"Yes." Janna's throat tightened with tears. "When

I was a child, it was our favorite place. We used to stay there for hours, just sitting and listening to the earth spirits whisper to us. Grandmother used to say that if I listened attentively enough to the wind and the trees and the earth, they would know me as their daughter and give me their strength." She drew a long, shaky breath. "Yes, I'm always with her there."

There was a brief pause, and when Jody spoke again, there was a suspicion of huskiness in his own voice. "It sure must have worked. You're one of the strongest people I know, Janna."

She closed her eyes and leaned her head against the wall. "Not strong enough," she said huskily. "I'm not as strong as she is, Jody. Sometimes I think that I can't bear it any longer without coming to her."

"She wouldn't see you, Janna," Jody said gently. "Your grandmother is a very determined lady, and this is the way she wants it. You're the most important person in her life. You know that. It's not because she doesn't love you that she won't have you with her now."

"I know. I know," Janna said tearfully. "It's just that she has so little time left now. I want to say goodbye, damn it."

"And that's just what she doesn't want," Jody said quietly. "She's right, and you know it. The two of you have the closest bond I've ever known between two individuals. Strong as she is, she couldn't stand experiencing your pain as well as her own. She wants to die with the same simple dignity that she's lived. You've got to give her that gift, Janna."

"I will, Jody," she said, over the lump in her throat. "I suppose I get a little desperate now and then, but I won't rob her of that. She still won't speak to me on the phone?"

"No, I asked her the last time you called," he said sympathetically. "She said there was nothing more to be said between you—that love needed no words, and goodbyes were meaningless, since she'd always be with you."

Janna drew a deep, shuddering breath. "She's not in any pain?" she asked softly.

He hesitated. "If she is, she doesn't talk about it," he said slowly. "But then, she wouldn't, would she?"

"No, she wouldn't," Janna agreed. She would just endure with that silent serenity that was so much a part of her. But she mustn't think about that. "Talk to me, Jody," Janna demanded throatily. "Tell me what she's been doing, everything she's said during the last three days."

It was her usual request, and Jody was ready for it. He had stored every incident and scrap of conversation and now poured them forth generously, so that she could envision the simple homelike scenes and feel as if she were once more a part of their life. When she rang off fifteen minutes later, she was inexpressibly soothed by the process, as she always was. Bless Jody.

His sympathy and understanding were making this agonizing ordeal almost bearable. Their conversation always tore her emotions to shreds, but she couldn't resist the opportunity to maintain even this ephemeral contact with her grandmother. She sat quite still, her eyes closed, breathing deeply and letting the serenity that her grandmother had taught her so long ago flow into her and gradually overwhelm the pain she was experiencing.

"Janna." Pat Dawson's voice was concerned. "Are you all right?"

She opened her eyes, too startled to veil their tear-bright agony, and Dawson muttered a swift imprecation beneath his breath. He squatted before her, frowning worriedly.

"What the hell is wrong?" he asked, taking her hands comfortingly in his own warm clasp. "Is there anything I can do to help?"

She instinctively clutched his hands with the desperation and desolation of a terrible loneliness. Then she slowly relaxed, and her lashes fell to veil her eyes. "No, there's nothing you can do," she said quietly. "There's nothing anyone can do, Pat." She leaned back in the chair, suddenly feeling drained and unutterably weary. "I'd rather not talk about it, if you don't mind."

"Whatever you say," Pat said slowly, his worried gaze narrowing on her face. "But sometimes it helps." His hands were absently running in soothing, caressing motions from her elbow to her wrist. "I'm always here if you need a shoulder to cry on."

"Thanks, I appreciate the offer," Janna replied gravely, smiling at him shakily. "I just may take you up on that sometime."

"Do that," he said, grinning. "I don't have five sisters for nothing. I've gotten quite accomplished at that sort of thing."

"Dawson!" The name had the explosive crack of a whiplash, and they both looked up, startled, at Santine's taut, menacing figure standing in the open doorway of the library.

Pat Dawson's hands fell from her arms as if they'd been burned, and he jumped hurriedly to his feet. Janna really couldn't blame him for being disconcerted. Santine looked more angry than she'd ever seen him. His dark eyes were stormy in a face that was all the more intimidating for its rigid control.

"Yes, Mr. Santine?" Pat inquired hastily, trying to regain a modicum of dignity.

"If you can manage to tear yourself away from Janna, there are some figures on my desk I want you to phone into the San Francisco office," Santine said between his teeth.

"Tonight?" Dawson asked, startled.

"If it's not too much trouble," Santine said caustically, his brows drawing together in a ferocious frown.

"No, of course not," Dawson replied hurriedly, striding swiftly toward the library. "Shall I call you if they have any questions?"

Santine's blazing eyes were now fixed on Janna, and the fury in them caused her to catch her breath. "Handle it yourself," he said. "I don't want to be bothered tonight."

Dawson disappeared into the library and closed the door quietly behind him.

The door had hardly shut when Santine was striding explosively toward Janna, his rigid control gone.

"Did you think I was too preoccupied to notice your little clandestine rendezvous?" Santine asked hoarsely. He was breathing hard, his usually bronze face flushed, and Janna felt a little thrill of fear race down her spine. "First you slipping out of the room, and then Dawson following a discreet time later." He reached down, fastened one iron hand around her wrist, and jerked her to her feet. "I'm not that much of a fool, Janna. It was more than obvious what you were up to."

Janna's eyes widened in shock. "No," she protested faintly. "You're wrong. It wasn't like that."

"Wasn't it?" Santine's lips curved in a savage smile. "And I suppose he didn't have his hands all over you when I came through the door. I would have thought Dawson would have a little more discretion than to attempt to seduce you in such a public place. I fully expected to have to track you to his bedroom."

Janna moistened her lips nervously. "He wasn't trying to seduce me," she said shakily. "You don't understand."

"I understand that you were as docile and willing as a common whore while he had his hands on you," he said thickly, his black eyes blazing into her face. "But what else should I expect? You're no different from any other woman in that respect. Was Dawson going to be just another of your 'simple biological couplings,' or did you feel something special for him?"

His deep, sandpaper voice was an enraged snarl as he uttered the last question. Without waiting for an answer, he turned and strode swiftly through the foyer, dragging her behind him. Then Janna was struggling to maintain her balance as he swiftly mounted the stairs.

"Where are we going?" she asked bewilderedly, trying to keep up with him.

He had reached the top of the stairs and was dragging her behind him down the long corridor. Then he threw open a door and pulled her into the bedroom and slammed the door behind them.

Five

"I should think it would be fairly obvious," Santine said tersely, releasing her wrist to reach out and flick the light switch beside the door. There was no question of where she was. The huge master bedroom fairly breathed Rafe's boldly masculine presence, with its plush white carpet and oversized furniture, upholstered in rich black velvet. A massive, king-sized canopy bed was draped with matching ebony velvet and gave a vaguely medieval atmosphere to the room. "It appears you have certain needs that aren't being met, and I assure you that if you're going to 'couple' with anyone, it's going to be with me."

Janna drew a deep breath, and her brown eyes were steady on his. "You're making a mistake," she said quietly. "Will you let me explain?"

His lips twisted cynically. "I'm not in the mood for explanations, I'm afraid," he said bitterly. He shrugged. "It was only a matter of time until we reached this point anyway. I've never been one to turn my back on something I want, and I've been aching to have you in my bed since the moment I saw you."

"But you said in—"

"I don't give a damn what I said," he interrupted. His voice was rough, and his dark eyes flickered restlessly. "All I know is that I want you, and I'm not about to let anyone else have you." His eyes narrowed. "Unless you wish to renege on our agreement."

She bit her lip and, looking into his face, she could see that there was nothing she could say that would change his mind. Perhaps he was right, she thought wearily; perhaps they would have reached this point sooner or later anyway. They both had been aware of the sexual tension that had subtly colored every word and glance since that night at the gazebo. Considering Santine's possessively jealous nature, it was a wonder he had maintained control as long as this.

She shook her head slowly. "No, I won't go back on my word," she said quietly. "If that's what you want."

"Oh, that's what I want," he said, smiling mirthlessly. "It may not be what's wise or sane, but it's definitely what I want." He bent forward, and his lips hovered for an instant over her own before he drew a deep, shuddering breath and took an abrupt step back. "I can't touch you right now. There's a thread of violence in me, and you seem to set it off without the least effort." His lips curved with savage cynicism. "You may deserve it, but for some reason I don't want to hurt you tonight." He turned and strode across the room, ripping off the black sport coat and scarlet sweater as he did so. "So we'll indulge in a little foreplay until I cool down a bit." He laughed shortly and threw the sweater and jacket carelessly on the black velvet easy chair next to the canopy bed. "Rather ironic, when foreplay is supposed to do just the opposite, isn't it?" He sat down on the end of the bed, and his eyes narrowed on her still figure across the room. "Come here, Janna."

Janna took a deep breath before moving quietly across the room to stand docilely before him, trying to keep her expression serene. It didn't prove to be the easiest thing to do, with Santine sitting there with the indolent arrogance of a sultan summoning

his favorite harem girl. Naked to the waist, his powerfully muscled chest and massive, brawny shoulders gleamed and rippled under the overhead light
like beaten copper, and the curly dark hair on his
chest was curiously inviting to touch. She must
have succeeded, however, for his mouth twisted
bitterly. "So meek and willing," he said harshly,
black eyes flaming savagely. "And so damn determined to save your precious animals. You'd do anything I'd ask you to, wouldn't you? Anything."

For some reason her docility seemed to be goading
him to even greater anger. "Yes, anything," she said
simply, and he muttered a violent obscenity that
caused her eyes to widen in surprise.

He was suddenly on his feet, his hands at his belt.
"Well, damn it, you're going to be called upon to
demonstrate that willingness tonight," he said tersely,
swiftly stripping off the rest of his clothes. "I've been
lying in that bed for a week, as sleepless and aching
as a schoolboy who's just discovered sex. I've had
time to weave quite a few fantasies around you,
Janna, and before you leave here you're going to
satisfy every one."

He moved away to toss the rest of his clothes on
top of his jacket and sweater on the chair, and
Janna's eyes followed him with irresistible fascination. There was nothing graceful or sculptured about
Santine's naked body, yet it was beautiful all the
same. Everything about it was massive and powerful,
from the sturdy column of his thighs and tight buttocks to the hard, flat stomach. He was all sleek,
virile power, and strength. Then, as he turned and
strode back to her, there was a tense readiness about
that strength that made Janna catch her breath.

Santine's eyes followed her gaze down his body,
and he smiled mockingly. "As you see, our foreplay
may not be as long as I'd like," he said softly. "But
there's time for a few of those fantasies to be realized before I lose total control." Still without touch-

ing her, he lay down across the end of the king-sized bed, raising himself on one elbow and gazing at her with the same arrogant indulgence she'd noticed earlier. "Undress for me, Janna. Very slowly."

"I'm afraid you'll be very disappointed in my performance," she said with a coolness that she was far from feeling. "I've never done a striptease before." Her hands were on the velvet sash at her waist, and she made a conscious effort to still their trembling as she untied it and dropped it on the cream carpet at her feet.

"I won't be disappointed," he said thickly, his dark eyes fixed compulsively on the graceful fingers that were now unfastening the tiny pearl buttons of her tailored white silk blouse. "My fantasy wasn't of some cheap sideshow, Janna." She had finished unbuttoning the front of the blouse, and she lifted one arm to unbutton the cuff. "God, I love to watch you move. It gives me an almost sensual pleasure to see you gesture with those lovely hands or merely walk across the room." There was a fitful gleam in the depths of Santine's eyes, and he spoke almost to himself. "I'll be giving instructions to Dawson or talking on the phone and you'd get up and stroll across the library to get a book from a shelf or stand in front of the window looking out at the courtyard. I have to force myself not to stare at you like a love-sick adolescent."

Janna silently slipped off the blouse and dropped it on the floor beside the sash. She unbuttoned the emerald velvet evening skirt and let it slide in a pool of jewel-bright color about her ankles before stepping out of it. Suddenly she was no longer nervous. Santine's words oddly had robbed the situation of any hint of tawdriness. She felt only a curious remoteness that was almost dreamlike as she deftly undressed as casually as if there were no Rafe Santine watching her with burning intentness. As she undid the front closing of her bra and shrugged out of it, she heard his sharply indrawn breath, but she tranquilly ignored it as she slipped out of her medium-heeled sandals. As usual, she hadn't worn stockings, and white satin bikini panties were the only stitch left on her body. Then they were also gone, and she raised her head to gaze at the man before her with serene pride. Nudity had never been shameful or dirty to her, and she took pleasure in the firm, graceful strength of her body. Nor was the intensity of Santine's regard shameful or degrading. There was only hot, eager desire and an element of almost pained pleasure in his expression as his gaze ran over her with lingering thoroughness. "Beautiful," he rasped hoarsely. "Slim and graceful and proud. I knew you'd look like this."

His dark gaze was on the fullness of her breasts, and Janna could feel them swell and tauten beneath his eyes as if his lips were once more caressing them as they had in the gazebo. She felt a slow liquid languor in the pit of her stomach, and suddenly she was finding it hard to get her breath. "What now?" she asked faintly, trying to hide the effect he was having on her.

"Walk across the room and then come here to me," he said thickly as he slowly sat up and swung his feet to the floor. "I want to watch the lovely music you make and know that soon you'll be moving under me with that same wild beauty."

She obediently turned and strode to the far end of the room; whirling, she moved much more slowly back to where he sat on the bed. Her heart was beating so hard now that she was sure he would be able to hear it when she stopped a few feet from him. She was suddenly unbearably shy.

"No, closer," he said huskily. Parting his legs he reached out his hand to clasp her wrist and draw her gently forward between them. His massive body was taut as a bowstring and she could see a bead of moisture on his forehead as he slowly lowered his head to rest it lightly against the soft cushion of her breasts. His hands slid with utmost care around her waist, as though he were afraid she would break if he exerted the slightest pressure. "Oh, Lord, I ache for you," he murmured, closing his eyes and brushing his dark head back and forth against her naked breasts in a nestling movement that was ambivalently passionate and boyish. "Help me, Janna. I need you so much, I'm hurting."

The plea served to move her as a harsher demand would not have, and Janna experienced an almost maternal tenderness as her arms slipped around his sturdy bronze neck and her hands tangled in the heavy crispness of his hair. She held him to her breasts and rocked him there, cradling his head against her softness, while her hands in his hair stroked and gentled him as if he were a child in pain. "I will, Rafe," she crooned softly. "I will." Her lips brushed tenderly against his moist forehead. "Tell me what you want me to do."

His arms tightened around her waist with a spasmodic force that took her breath away. "Little earth mother," he choked hoarsely. "My lovely little earth mother." She could feel him shudder against her and she felt a fierce primitive thrill at the thought that need for her could make this strong, dominant man tremble. Then they were both falling on the bed, Rafe's arms effortlessly cushioning her fall. With one swift movement he twisted her over so that she was lying on her back on the ebony velvet coverlet and he was bending over her, his eyes shining with fierce possession.

One finger reached out and gently touched the taut pinkness of her nipple. "God, what a gorgeous, dusky Indian maiden you are, Pocahontas," he said softly. "Even your hair is almost tan." His hand moved to the thick, lustrous braid lying on the curve of her breast.

His hands were working swiftly with the braid,

and it was only seconds before he was running his hands through the loosened tresses lying in a shining, rippling cloud on her shoulders. Then his face was buried in the silky mass while his hand closed possessively over her breast. "Mine," he muttered huskily as his lips moved in swift hot kisses on the line of her throat. "Don't ever wear your hair loose except when we're like this, Janna. I need to know that something about you is mine alone."

Then, before she could reply, his lips were parting hers and his tongue was claiming her own in a joust that robbed her of breath and sent a hot tingling through her loins. She made a sound that was half gasp, half moan, and her arms slid around his shoulders and pulled him to her in a fierce possessiveness that she wasn't even aware of in the heat of the moment. Rafe's lips left hers and were covering her throat and shoulders with tiny gentle kisses, alternating with an occasional tugging bite at the silky skin that was startlingly arousing.

But then, everything that Rafe was doing to her was arousing, Janna thought hazily as the lips moved down to nibble at the burgeoning hardness of her nipple. He spent a long time there, and she was soon panting and moving restlessly beneath him in a torment of need.

He raised his head and gazed down at her with glazed, feverish eyes. "That's right," he said thickly. "Move for me. Move to the music I'll play for you, Janna."

Suddenly he was on his knees and gathering her in his arms, moving her farther up on the bed. Then his hands were parting her legs, his fingers lazily caressing the inside of her thighs while he stared down at her with an odd expression of torment on his face. "Are you ready for me, Janna?" he asked hoarsely. "God, I wanted to wait until I was sure it would be good for you, but I don't think I can." He moved between her thighs and parted her legs still wider, his nails now teasing the soft, sensitive flesh with an abrasive rubbing motion. "I usually don't give a damn, but I wanted it to be so special for you this time."

Janna looked up at him dazedly, feeling more weak and vulnerable than she had ever before in her life. Every muscle and nerve in her body seemed to be aching, pulsating, with a need that only the man above her could satisfy. Only he could end this hot liquid ache that was tormenting her. "Rafe," she gasped, and it was all there in her voice. "Please."

A flash of exultant triumph illuminated his rough features, and he surged forward. "I'll take longer next time," he promised huskily. "I can't wait another second for you, Janna. I want you too much."

Then his warm hardness was within her and even the initial invasion was an assuagement of the frustrated need, but it wasn't enough. Not enough. Her hands clutched fiercely at Rafe's shoulders and tried to pull him closer to her. But for some maddening reason he was resisting her. "Easy," he said softly. "Relax, Janna. You're so tight, and I don't want to hurt you, baby. Don't tense up on me."

There wasn't anything tense about her, she thought wildly, her head twisting back and forth on the black velvet coverlet. She was all hot molten emptiness waiting to be filled, and it wasn't enough. She was unaware that her nails were digging into his shoulders, but he was still stubbornly withholding what she needed. Then, with an instinct as primitive as time itself, her hips surged forcefully upward to take what he would not give her. There was an instant of tearing pain that she scarcely noticed as she felt herself surrounding the full virile force of him with an explosion of almost savage pleasure, and the moan she gave at that moment was more of a guttural purr of satisfaction than of discomfort.

"My God!" Rafe breathed, freezing into statuelike stillness above her. Then, incredibly, he made an involuntary movement of withdrawal. But she wasn't about to give up what she'd won, and her legs instinctively curled around his hips, holding him to her. Nothing more was required, she discovered to her infinite satisfaction. Rafe muttered a low, broken imprecation that was almost a groan of pain and suddenly he was thrusting powerfully forward in a rhythm that took her breath away, stroking her with flaming need and fulfilling that need at one and the same time.

She wasn't conscious of how long the spiral of desire and fulfillment continued. She knew only it was essential that it did continue. That she move and thrust at Rafe's whispered urgings, that her hands and lips caress in a passionate exchange of favors, which also had an odd rhythm of their own, that she reach the final peak of white-hot pleasure just beyond her reach. Then she did reach it, with an electric forcefulness that left her devastated and trembling with shock. Then she heard Rafe's groan above her, his arms tightening about her, sealing their bodies together as if he were reluctant, even in satisfaction, to release the source of his pleasure.

His breath was coming in little jerks, his heart beating as wildly as her own. "Janna," he breathed huskily, his words stirring the soft tendrils of hair at her temple. "Oh, God, Janna."

She couldn't even get that much out. She felt as if she'd been whirling in the center of a hurricane. Every muscle felt weak and fluid, and she couldn't seem to stop trembling.

Without releasing her, Rafe rolled over so that they were facing each other. He reached over, plucking a fold of the coverlet, which pulled sideways, enveloping them both in its velvet prison. Then his hands once again slid beneath the cover to cup her buttocks and press their still-bound bodies into even greater intimacy.

"I don't want to let you go," he murmured, a trace

of wonder in his voice. "I'd like to wear you like a medallion and take you everywhere with me."

"That might be a trifle inconvenient," she said shakily, wishing she could regain a semblance of her usual serene composure.

One of Rafe's hands began a journey of exploration over her hip to the softness of her belly and then up to cup the fullness of her breast in his palm. There was a casual possessiveness in the action, as if he were merely reconnoitering territory that he'd already claimed, and suddenly Janna experienced a suffocating thrill of panic. She had the odd sensation that she was bound to him in more than body, that she was being absorbed into him, attached by cords stronger than steel, her spirit imprisoned as surely as if he had slammed the door of the cage behind her.

"Let me go," she whispered, trying to wriggle away from him.

His arms tightened around her, and his hand started a lazy kneading motion at her breast. "Presently," he murmured, nibbling at the lobe of her ear. "Perhaps in a week or two I might have had enough of you to let you out of bed long enough to eat a meal or go for a short stroll. But don't count on it." His tongue darted into her ear. "Definitely don't count on it."

She put her hand on his chest and pushed. "I want to go to my own room now." There must have been a thread of the panic she was feeling in her voice, for the lazy tenderness slowly faded from Rafe's face, and it hardened into its usual mocking cynicism. His arms tightened around her for a brief instant, and then he was pushing her away. He sat up and leaned indolently against the black velvet headboard.

"And what if I don't want you to go?" he asked harshly, watching her broodingly as she tossed the velvet coverlet aside and scooted to the opposite side of the bed. "What if I consider that I haven't had my fill of you tonight? Will you stay with me?"

She slipped out of bed and moved swiftly to the foot, where her clothes lay in disarray on the carpet. With every move away from him she was feeling more secure, more her own person. Nothing really irrevocable had happened, she assured herself desperately. It had all been an illusion brought on by that incredible physical and emotional experience she'd undergone. "Not tonight," she said, trying to keep her voice level. "I want to be alone now." She was dressing swiftly, eager to get away. "I'm not backing out of our agreement. I'll come to you tomorrow, if you like. I just need time to myself at the moment."

Rafe uttered an obscenity so violent that she looked up in surprise. His dark eyes were blazing stormily in his taut face. "Damn that agreement!" he said, his lips twisting bitterly. "Well, you warned me, didn't you, Janna? A simple biological coupling, and then you walk away with no resulting emotional hangups." She didn't answer, and he watched her, frowning, as she pulled on her blouse and started to button it. "Why didn't you tell me you were a virgin?"

"It didn't matter," Janna said absently as she tucked her blouse into her skirt.

"It mattered to me, damn it," he said moodily. "I've never had a virgin." His gaze traveled lingeringly over her. "I . . . liked it."

Janna kept her eyes lowered as she tied the sash about her waist. "I'm glad that I could provide you with a new experience," she said lightly, only half aware of what she was saying. Her entire body was throbbing with an aching sensitivity, and she was conscious of the swelling thrust of her breasts against the silk of her blouse. Was it happening again so soon? She wanted nothing more than to get back into bed and let Rafe show her once more how to satisfy that frustrating need, but she was beginning to realize how dangerous such an action could be. She glanced up briefly, her eyes guarded. "Perhaps I may be worth your two million dollars, after all."

For a moment she could have sworn there was a flash of pain in the depths of his eyes, but nothing showed in the implacable hardness of his face. "Perhaps," he said coolly. "We'll have to see. You still have a number of weeks to prove your value to me." He watched her with narrowed eyes as she slipped on her sandals. "So I'll waive my rights and privileges to that lovely body for the rest of the night. But I suggest you get the hell out of here before I change my mind."

She was already moving swiftly toward the door, and her hand was on the knob when he spoke again behind her.

"Janna!"

She paused, tensing, but didn't look back at him. She only wanted to escape, to run away from those velvet bonds he had manacled her with tonight.

"It wasn't just a simple biological coupling, damn it!" he said with soft violence. "Not for either of us."

Janna opened the door and swiftly left the bedroom.

Janna was not up at daybreak, as was her usual custom, the next morning, and was almost late for breakfast. She hadn't managed to go to sleep until dawn, despite her resolute attempts to do so. The privacy and solitude of her own space hadn't had the bracing effect that she'd hoped they would. She had felt a constant recurring physical desire for Rafe and a bewildering loneliness for him that she feared was not entirely of the flesh. This filled her with such unease it precluded any chance of sleep.

She couldn't permit herself any emotional response to Rafe Santine. Even disregarding the transient aspect to their relationship, she had no desire for a commitment to a man of Rafe's aggressive, dominant obsessiveness. He would be the worst possible choice for a woman with her own passionate need for freedom and independence. No, she couldn't possibly yield to that odd melting tenderness she was experiencing with increasing frequency of late. Now that she'd become Rafe's mistress, she was going to have to be constantly on guard to keep his physical magic from chipping away at her resistance. This firm resolution didn't prevent her heart giving a queer half skip when she saw Rafe sitting alone at the breakfast table on the terrace the next morning.

He looked up, frowning, as she came through the French doors. "You're late!" he said impatiently. He was dressed in black cords and a cream sweat shirt, with the sleeves pushed up carelessly to the elbow. He looked surprisingly boyish with that cross frown on his face, Janna thought as she slipped into her accustomed place opposite him.

"A little," she replied quietly, as she picked up her napkin. "Where are Pat and Diane this morning?"

"Dawson is very discreetly making himself scarce," Rafe said, his lips twisting sardonically. "He decided on a long walk in lieu of breakfast this morning." He poured her coffee from the silver pot by his plate. After replacing it he said, "Diane's gone."

"Gone?" Janna looked up, startled.

Rafe's scowl became darker. "She left early this morning," he said curtly. "She wasn't needed any more, so I sent her away." His lips twisted cynically. "I assure you that she wasn't tossed cruelly out in the cold. She received a quite generous stipend."

Janna bit her lip, her face troubled. "I don't doubt your generosity," she said slowly. "It just never occurred to me that you'd send her away. It's not as if I'm going to be here for more than a few weeks, and our agreement never called for any exclusive commitment on your part."

"My God, you're incredible," he said bitterly, his black eyes flickering. "Did you expect me to behave like some Middle Eastern sultan and call one or the other of you to my bed as the whim moved me?" His laugh was totally mirthless. "You probably did, at that. What the hell difference would it make to you? You'd accept it as coolly as you do the actual fact of occupying my bed."

Coolly? There had been nothing in the least cool about her response in Rafe's arms last night. "I don't think you're being quite fair," she said quietly. "I was only pointing out that you have no obligation to me in any way. If you want Diane here, I have—"

"Damn it, I don't want her," he grated out savagely. "I haven't wanted her from the moment I saw you. Do you think I didn't try to use her to wipe you out of my mind? It didn't work. She left me cold as ice. I might just as well have been a eunuch." His lips twisted. "So until I can rid myself of this aberration, you'll have to resign yourself to my exclusive attentions."

Janna tried to stifle the sudden surge of joy that shot through her at his words. What was the use of all her safe, sensible admonitions, when she couldn't control this almost primitive satisfaction at the elimination of a possible rival for Santine's affections? She lifted her untouched coffee to her lips, the long sweep of her lashes veiling her eyes. "I see," she said, as impersonally as she could manage. "Then I gather I've inherited Diane's role?"

"Did you think we could go back to the status quo after last night?" he asked dryly. "We were fantastic together, and I've never been one to deny myself after just one taste. I've ordered your clothes moved into my room."

Janna moistened her lips nervously as she felt again that panicky sensation of being boxed in. "I don't see why that's necessary," she said tautly. "Your former mistress had her own quarters and you appeared to be quite happy with the arrangement."

"But as you've pointed out, I'm only going to have your services for a limited amount of time," he said silkily. "I intend to reap the benefits of your charming presence while I may."

"But I don't—"

"You're moving in with me," he interrupted flatly, rising to his feet and throwing his napkin carelessly on the table. "Now, finish your breakfast while I go to the library and leave a few instructions for Dawson. Meet me in the courtyard in forty-five minutes. I want to be on our way by noon."

"Where are we going?" Janna asked, her eyes wide with surprise. She looked down at her chocolate denim jeans and beige tailored blouse. "Will I have to change?"

He shook his head. "What you have on will be fine," he said. "We're just going to take the helicopter down to the Camino Real Estate property."

"Camino Real . . . ?" Then her face cleared and her eyes lit up. "You mean we're going to the wildlife reserve?"

"Now that you've made the ultimate sacrifice, I thought you'd at least like to see what you've bought with your nubile young body," he said sardonically. "There are several buildings on the property. You might want to see if any of them could be of some use to you."

"Oh, yes," Janna said eagerly, jumping to her feet. "Could we go right away?"

"I didn't see that much enthusiasm on Diane's face when I gave her a sapphire necklace," Rafe said, his lips quirking in amusement. Then he frowned. "And no, we can't go right now. You haven't eaten breakfast yet, damn it." His gaze went over her impatiently. "You're thin as a rail. I don't want you to meet me in the courtyard until you've had an egg, toast, bacon, and some fruit, not that skimpy toast and coffee you usually insist upon," he ended sternly. "Understand?"

She grinned happily, and nodded as she reached briskly for the eggs. "Right."

He stood watching her for a brief moment as she obediently dished up the stipulated food, and there was an odd flicker of tenderness in his usually hard face. Then he moved reluctantly toward the French doors, and as he passed her chair, he gave her braid an affectionate little tug. "Good girl," he said gruffly. He was gone before she could reply.

Six

Rafe gave her a complete aerial tour of the property designated for the reserve, pointing out landmarks and boundaries with an efficiency and knowledge that was astounding. But the loud whine of the rotors of the helicopter prevented any in-depth conversation, and it was only after they'd landed in a clearing a short distance from a large clapboard farmhouse and a cluster of outbuildings, that Janna was able to satisfy her curiosity.

As they made their way toward the farmhouse, she looked up at Rafe, her face puzzled. "How do you know so much about this particular property? It can't be standard procedure for a businessman of your stature to be so thoroughly versed in a minor real estate investment."

His dark brows arched mockingly. "I'm glad you're suitably impressed," he said with a boyish grin that amazingly softened the hardness of his face. "I admit to doing my homework. After we'd concluded our little arrangement, I ordered both an aerial and ground survey of the entire property, complete with photos. I thought it might prove useful to you to know the location of every cave and possible watering place on the acreage. It won't be all that easy to keep track of your four-footed charges on a reserve this size. Dawson has all the maps and photos on file. You can ask him for them when you get back."

"Thank you, I will," Janna said dazedly, darting a

glance at his face. It was an amazingly thoughtful thing for Rafe to have done, when he'd claimed to have no interest in the project. "It will be a tremendous help to us."

A further surprise awaited her at the farmhouse. After unlocking the front door, Santine took her elbow protectively. "Watch your step," he warned tersely. "This is Sunday, and there won't be any workmen here, but they may have left some of their tools and equipment about."

"Workmen?" Janna asked as she entered into what must previously have been a foyer. Now it was hard to tell what it was. There was evidence of demolition and reconstruction everywhere. The walls that had separated the different rooms had been completely torn down, and there were tools and ladders lying carelessly throughout the area, as Rafe had guessed. "What's going on here?"

"Since this is the largest building, I thought it would be the logical choice for your veterinary clinic and research facilities," Santine said abstractedly, striding forward to examine the work on a window that had been enlarged to encompass almost an entire wall. Evidently the workmanship met with his approval, and he turned toward her with frank enjoyment at the stunned surprise on her face.

"Your medical and laboratory equipment will arrive next week. Dawson consulted the San Diego Zoo, and they furnished him with a complete list of what they thought you'd need. If there's anything we've missed, just tell Dawson and he'll order it." He took out a small notebook from his back pocket and flipped it open. "There's a Dr. Martin Buckley at the Johannesburg Zoo, who's had considerable success with artificial insemination in endangered species when all else fails. I thought he might prove useful to you, but he won't be able to relocate for another three months. Will that be satisfactory?"

"Quite satisfactory," Janna said faintly, her eyes

wide with shock, looking around her helplessly. It was a gift of such enormous generosity, it fairly staggered her. She was impressed, not so much by the expense involved, but by the care and planning that had gone into what Rafe was offering her so casually. "It's everything we could possibly want." Her eyes were fixed bewilderedly on him across the room. "But why?"

There was an oddly embarrassed expression on Rafe's face. "If you're going to do something, you might as well do it right," he said gruffly. His eyes slid guiltily away from hers, as if he were a small boy caught in some mischief. He turned and gestured briskly to the stairs leading up to the second floor. "I've ordered the upper floor to be converted into an apartment for your Dr. Sandler. I figured he'd want to be on the spot in case of any medical problems."

"Yes, he would," Janna replied absently as she moved slowly across the room toward Rafe, her gaze fixed in fascination on his face. There was a definite flush on his swarthy skin, she noticed with amazement. Yes, the suave buccaneer of the boardroom was definitely *not* composed. She stopped when she was only a foot away and looked searchingly into his face. "Why, Rafe?" she repeated softly. "It's too much. I can't believe that anyone could be that fanatic a perfectionist."

He scowled crossly into the glowing face gazing up at him, and almost compulsively one hand lifted to touch the smooth contour of her cheek. "Didn't you ever hear the maxim, 'Never look a gift horse in the mouth'?" he asked caustically. "What the hell difference does it make why I did it?"

"It matters," Janna said quietly, standing quite still beneath his hand that was stroking her cheek. "It matters very much."

His fingers traced the curve of her brow. "It was those doe eyes," he growled, his voice again like sandpaper velvet and a fierce frown darkening his face. "That night you saw Sylvia Waterman's tiger-skin coat, you looked like Bambi after his mother was shot. I couldn't take it." He glared at her accusingly. "And then you *cried.*"

"You did all this just because I cried?" Janna asked blankly, with a gesture that encompassed both the room and the totality of his actions.

"I told you that I couldn't take it," he grated out, squaring his jaw belligerently. "I'm not used to just standing by and doing nothing when I want something fixed. It frustrated the hell out of me to know I couldn't heal your pain no matter what I did." He shrugged helplessly. "Hell, I even offered you Waterman and his wife's heads on a silver platter and you turned that down too."

Janna's lips twisted in amusement at the outraged disgust on Rafe's face. "I didn't mean to appear ungrateful," she said soberly, her brown eyes twinkling. "I've just never found revenge particularly rewarding."

His hand had moved from her face and was now playing with her braid. He gave it a sharp admonitory tug. "It's all that blasted idealism," he said gruffly, but with a surprisingly tender curve to his lips. "If you lived in the real world, you'd know revenge can be very sweet indeed." There was almost an abashed expression on his face as he asked softly, "Do you like your present, Pocahontas?"

Janna could feel her throat tighten, and her eyes misted with tears. "I love my present, Rafe," she said shakily, trying to smile. "If this was meant to heal my hurt, you certainly know how to apply a very impressive bandage." She turned her head, and pressed a lingering kiss on the hand that was wrapped around her braid. "Thank you."

"Oh, hell, you're not going to cry again," he protested disgustedly.

She laughed huskily, experiencing that same melting tenderness. "No, I'm not going to cry again,"

she assured him throatily, and immediately a tear
brimmed over and ran down her cheek.

He pulled a handkerchief out of his pocket and
dabbed vigorously at her brimming eyes. "I should
have known better than to trust a woman's word,"
he said, with a gloomy sigh. "This is where I came
in. What will it take this time to make you stop?"
His lips twisted wryly. "I suppose I could put all my
resources into finding a method to make Tibetan
panda bears reproduce. Would that make you happy?"

"Oh, Rafe." His name was half laugh, half sob,
and the tears started to flow faster than ever.

Rafe muttered an imprecation and pulled her swiftly
into his arms, one hand holding her face buried in
the soft fleecy material of his sweat shirt. His heartbeat was strong and steady beneath her ear, and he
smelled deliciously of the clean fragrance of soap
and the faint woodsy tang of cologne.

"Lord, what am I going to do with you?" Rafe
murmured softly, rocking her tenderly. "Why couldn't
you have picked someone else's wall to climb over?
My life was so simple before you came along. I don't
want to feel like this, damn it." His hand was gently
massaging her nape. "I lied to you when I told you
that I'd never had a pet. None of the foster homes I
was in would let me have a cat or a dog, but there
was a little gray-and-white kitten I found living in a
cardboard box in an alley. I couldn't bring it home,
but I'd feed her every day, and it got so she would
run to meet me every time I turned into the alley.
Then one day the kitten didn't come to meet me,
and I never saw it again. I think I missed that kitten
more than I did my mother when she deserted me.
That kitten was *mine*, damn it. She had no right to
go away." His arms tightened around her. "I never
felt like that about anyone or anything again, until I
saw you that night in the study. I've never felt tenderness for a woman before or wanted to protect
her. I certainly never felt it necessary to have a woman

beside me constantly for companionship as well as sex." His voice was oddly husky. "I'm scared as hell, Janna. Because some day I'm going to turn around and you're not going to be there either. I won't let you do that to me."

Janna tried to lift her head, but he held it firmly pressed to his shoulder. "No, don't move," he said softly. "I like to feel you all weak and cuddly in my arms. "You're so blasted strong and self-reliant that I won't get this opportunity very often."

She didn't really want to move, and she relaxed against his hard warmth with a sigh of contentment. The next few moments were almost dreamlike as they stood wrapped in each other's arms in an intimacy free from all desires or demands, giving and partaking only of the warmth of their bodies. She didn't want to let herself think of the words Rafe had just spoken. They revealed an unexpected vulnerability she'd never suspected in a man of his tough ruthlessness, and that vulnerability was far more dangerous to her than Rafe's undisputed sexual expertise. Each word had seemed to forge another link in the chain that was beginning to bind them together, a chain Rafe was also obviously struggling to sever.

"Shall I go away?" she asked quietly, after a long quiet moment in his arms.

"It's too late for that," he answered slowly, and she felt the soft brush of a kiss on her brow. "We'll just have to ride it out. Maybe it really is only a temporary aberration." He pushed her away and looked gravely into her face. "I sure as hell hope so." His arms dropped from around her, and he turned and glanced out the window again. "It's clouding up. I think we're going to have a storm," he commented abruptly.

"Should we get back to the Castle?" Janna asked, her eyes following his to the lowering darkness in the west. "Will it be dangerous flying the helicopter?"

"There's no immediate hurry," he said casually, sliding an arm around her waist and turning her toward the door. "It appears to be moving fairly slowly. We may even have time to get in our picnic before it hits. There's a lake about a half mile from here that looks like an ideal spot."

It was also a very beautiful spot, Janna thought contentedly thirty minutes later, as she unpacked the food from the picnic hamper and placed it on a gold, brown, and white plaid blanket. The lake was very small but amazingly clear, shimmering like mother of pearl under the rapidly graying skies and mirroring the tall verdant pines and oaks surrounding it.

"It's really lovely here, isn't it?" Janna asked softly as her gaze traveled contentedly around the bucolic panorama before her. "Southern California has almost everything."

"Almost?" Rafe asked, his brow arching mockingly. "There are Californians who would argue about that qualification." He was sprawled lazily across from her, leaning against a boulder, and he reached for a crusty piece of chicken as he spoke.

"I miss the seasons," Janna said, pouring coffee from the thermos into paper cups. She handed one across to him and then poured one for herself. "This time of year at home the trees are ablaze with color." Her brown eyes were warm with memories as she lifted the coffee to her lips. "There's a hill on our farm that's absolutely fantastic when the leaves have turned. The hues are so brilliant it hurts you to look at them. Every fall my grandmother and I used to gather baskets of leaves and bring them home to decorate the house. She was wonderful with any kind of floral arrangement."

His dark eyes were thoughtful on her face. "You and your grandmother are very close, aren't you?" he asked idly.

Janna nodded. "Very close," she said quietly. "She's

been my friend, my teacher, almost my other half, from the time I could toddle around after her. We had a rapport so strong that most of the time we didn't even need words."

"What about your father?" Rafe asked. "Were you equally close to him?"

Janna's face clouded. "No. I think perhaps he tried after my mother died, but he could never really understand either of us." She shrugged. "Perhaps he didn't want to. I think he was a little ashamed of having a Cherokee Indian mother. Even today being a half-breed in a white world can be very difficult."

"It must have been considerably worse for your grandmother," Rafe said speculatively. "I'm surprised she even had the courage to leave her people to marry your grandfather."

Janna lowered her lashes to veil the sudden mistiness of her eyes. "Oh, she has plenty of courage," she said throatily. "She's the bravest lady I know." Her lips curved bitterly. "But it didn't take any great amount of courage for her to leave the reservation." She glanced over at Rafe inquiringly. "Have you ever visited an Indian reservation?" When he shook his head, she said soberly, "I have. My grandmother took me to the one where she grew up, when I was a small child." She shivered. "It was like a concentration camp. The boundaries were even marked with barbed-wire fencing. I don't know how she was able to bear it." Her face was shadowed with memories. "She couldn't ever stand to be confined. As long as I can remember, weather permitting, she's slept on the screened-in porch that runs along the back of the house. She said she couldn't breathe penned up within walls. I think she would have died if she'd had to stay on that reservation."

Santine straightened slowly, a frown creasing his forehead. "Aren't you being a little melodramatic?" he asked, his lips tightening. He threw the half-eaten piece of chicken aside. "If she's as strong as you say, she might have adjusted quite happily to the loss of freedom. How do you know that she wouldn't have found compensations?"

Her eyes widened at his vehemence. Why was he so angry? "Because I know her," she faltered. "Nothing could have compensated for what she'd have lost."

"You can't be sure of that," Rafe said moodily. He cast a restless glance at the sky, which was rapidly turning from gray to a stormy blue-black. "Come on," he said abruptly as he knelt and started throwing the remains of their lunch haphazardly back into the picnic basket. "That storm's going to cut loose any minute. We'd better try to find some shelter."

They were only halfway back to the farmhouse when the first drops began to fall. It was quickly followed by a deluge, which soaked them both to the skin in a matter of minutes. Rafe grabbed her elbow and propelled her into a brisk sprint that brought them quickly in sight of the farmhouse. But instead of making for the house itself, he stopped at the door of the barn and pulled her into its dim, musty shelter.

"This is closer," Rafe said in answer to the inquiring glance she shot him. "And the workmen haven't started renovation here as yet. There's a chance we may be able to find a blanket or some old clothes to dry off with." He frowned as his gaze went over her soaked figure. "You're completely drenched."

"So are you," she said lightly, trying to catch her breath after their run from the lake. "I think we'll both survive." She grinned happily. "Personally, I feel great." The sprint through the cold clean rain had sent the blood tingling through her veins, and she felt glowingly alive, despite the fact she probably resembled a drowned puppy.

Rafe put a hand to her cheek. "You're cold," he said curtly, his hand falling away as he turned to survey the interior of the barn. "And once your pulse rate slows down, you're going to begin to feel it. We've got to get you dry." He was walking briskly between the stalls. "Open the door; it's dark as Hades in here."

Janna obediently threw wide the double doors of the barn before following him. He was at the far side of the barn when she joined him, and judging by his expression, what he'd discovered hadn't pleased him.

"Clean as a whistle," he said wryly. "Not so much as a moth-eaten old horse blanket. The entire place is practically sterile."

"I told you it didn't matter," Janna said quickly. "Why don't we just make a run for the helicopter and wait it out there?"

"And by the time the weather clears enough to take off you'd probably have a hell of a chill," he said curtly, still looking searchingly around the barn. Suddenly his gaze fell upon a ladder leading up to the hayloft. "Bingo," he said softly. He patted Janna's extremely wet derriere. "Up you go. I'll be there in a minute." He strode briskly toward the front of the barn.

Janna gazed after him for an instant before she turned with a rueful shrug and started to climb the ladder to the loft. Rafe was very quick, and she'd barely reached the confines of the loft when he was ascending the ladder behind her, carrying the picnic hamper, which he'd dropped by the barn door when they ran in from the storm.

Janna moved away from the ladder and sank to her knees in the soft cushion of hay, watching Rafe as he swung lithely off the top step of the ladder. He squatted beside her and opened the hamper. "We'll have to make do with the materials we have on hand," he said as he rifled hastily through the basket. He scowled disgustedly. "God knows there appear to be few enough of them in here."

Janna's lips quirked. "It's a picnic hamper, not a

nuclear survival kit," she said demurely, her brown eyes twinkling.

"Very amusing," he said dryly, glancing up at her. "I wonder if you'll prove as entertaining with a lousy head cold." He snapped the hamper shut and pushed it aside. "One blanket, one tablecloth, eight napkins, and four paper towels."

"Pretty good, considering," Janna said blithely, sitting back on her heels. "That's obviously a picnic hamper fit for a billionaire. My picnic lunches usually consist of a sandwich stuck in a paper bag."

"Come here," he ordered briskly, and when she edged closer so that she was facing him, he picked up one of the gold, brown, and white plaid napkins and began to pat her face dry. "Knowing you, that probably suited you right down to the ground," he said absently. He wiped away the dampness from her nape. "Nothing to keep you from moving on once you'd finished your meal, and nothing to take along with you either." His hands were rapidly unbraiding her hair.

"Well, it's definitely more convenient when I'm out on the reserve," she admitted as his hands threaded themselves through her loosened hair and combed through it briskly.

"Your hair isn't as wet as I thought," Rafe said idly, throwing the damp napkin aside and picking up another one. He separated a long silky tress and began to dry it with the cloth. "Some of it must have been protected by the braiding."

Janna sat as docilely as a child while he quickly went over her hair, strand by strand, with the cloth. The intimate attention Rafe was showing her made her feel treasured and protected, and she had no desire to lose that feeling by asserting her independence in what would be a purely symbolic display. Then she was abruptly jarred out of her narcissistic contentment as she noticed a drop of moisture running down Rafe's cheek from his still-wet hair. He was the one who'd been ill, she thought guiltily. Yet she was selfishly sitting here letting him take care of *her*.

She grabbed up a napkin and edged still closer. "Now it's my turn," she said firmly, wiping his face gently with the cloth. "You're far wetter than I am." She rubbed at the heavy sideburns, frowning in concentration. "You have a little silver in your hair," she observed casually. "I've never noticed that before."

"It's probably a new acquisition," he said, his voice oddly husky. "I'm sure it wasn't there before you appeared on the scene."

Janna laughed softly, her gaze leaving his hair to glance down into his eyes. What she saw there caused her to catch her breath and her hands to halt in their task. She was suddenly acutely aware of how close she was to the vibrant heat of his body. Mere inches separated them, and her arms were lifted on each side of his head in an intimate parody of an embrace. "Perhaps you'd better finish yourself," she said faintly, making a move to lower her hands from his hair.

He caught her upper arms in his hands, preventing her from completing the motion. "No," he said softly, his eyes holding hers with a mesmerizing intimacy. "Keep on with it. I like your hands on me."

Janna looked away hurriedly and with dreamlike slowness continued with her task, hardly conscious of what she was doing. She was only aware of the slow rise and fall of Rafe's chest as he breathed in and out and the pulse beating strongly at the side of his throat. With every breath she could smell that woodsy cologne, the freshness of the rain, and the musty sweetness of the loose hay that surrounded them. There was no noise but the drumming of the rain on the roof of the barn and the light sound of their own breathing. The silence seemed to quicken her own awareness to an almost painful sensitivity.

It was as if she could feel each individual straw of the soft, fragrant mass they were kneeling upon through the fabric of her jeans, and she was suddenly conscious of the ripe heaviness of her breasts as they brushed against Rafe with the movement of her hands in his hair.

"That's enough," Rafe said thickly.

Her arms fell slowly to her sides. Her gaze flew back to the hot intensity of his, and she moistened her lips nervously. "Do you think you're dry enough now?" she faltered.

He gave a short, mirthless laugh. "Don't worry about that," he said dryly. "I feel as if I'm generating enough heat at the moment to turn a rain forest into a virtual Sahara Desert." He drew a deep, shaky breath, and his gaze traveled over her lingeringly. "I wish that you'd let me finish before you decided to return the favor. You've made things difficult as hell, Pocahontas." His lips twisted wryly. "Now let's see how long my resistance will last before I throw you down in the hay and have my way with you."

"There's no need for you to bother," she said a trifle breathlessly as she started to edge away from him. "I'm dry as toast now."

"Sit still," he ordered raggedly, brushing a strand of silky hair away from her forehead. "Didn't anyone ever tell you there's nothing more provocative to a man's hunting instincts than a gazelle in flight? I'm not going to hurt you, damn it." Suddenly his eyes darkened with concern. "I didn't hurt you last night, did I?"

She could feel the warm color flood her face, and she shook her head vigorously.

"That's good," he said quietly, his expression relieved. "I meant to be more gentle when I found out you were a virgin, but you felt so hot and sweet that I went a little crazy."

He wasn't the only one, Janna thought wryly as he began to dry her throat. At that point she'd had no use for gentleness or restraint and had wanted only the pounding rhythm that had been the center of her universe. Just the memory of that moment brought a heavy languor to her loins and caused her nipples to harden and thrust against the wet fabric of her shirt.

Rafe could hardly miss the evidence of her arousal, and she heard his swift indrawn breath as he looked down at the swollen fullness of her breasts.

"God help me," he breathed softly, and slowly started to unbutton her shirt. His face was all blade-hard planes and contours, but his lips were beautifully sensual and his eyes midnight-dark with desire. His hands were trembling a little as he peeled the wet beige shirt off her. The flimsy bra followed immediately, and he stood looking at her for a long moment, his face flushed and his eyes glazed with intensity. "Lord, that's lovely," he said hoarsely. "There's nothing more beautiful in the world than a woman's breasts pleading to be loved." He rubbed the napkin over the taut nipples, the crisp abrasiveness of the cotton on their sensitive tips causing Janna to shiver and catch her breath. Then the cloth was moving over her midriff and around to the small of her back, so that she was enfolded in the curve of his arm, her breasts arched upward against him as he slowly moved the napkin in sensuous circles up and down her back. "I'm getting you wet again," he said softly, and, releasing her for a brief instant, he pulled his cream sweat shirt over his head and threw it carelessly aside. "Now, where were we?"

Janna reached out with one tentative hand to stroke the springy dark hair on the massive bronze chest. It felt deliciously abrasive against her soft palm. She could feel Rafe stiffen and then freeze beneath her hand, but she was too intrigued with her explorations to really notice. Her hand lightly traced the smooth, rippling muscles beneath the taut skin and then curiously sought out the small male nipples. Did they react to stimuli like her own, she wondered dreamily? Then she was irresistibly drawn to find out. She leaned forward, and her tongue darted out to caress the hard nub teasingly. She received her answer immediately in the form of Rafe's sharply indrawn breath and, encouraged, she transferred her attention to the other nipple, with similar success.

"You know that you're driving me out of my mind, of course," Rafe said, gasping, as her hands traced slowly from his chest to the hard flat muscles of his abdomen and stroked the taut smooth flesh with sensuous enjoyment. Janna didn't answer, as her teeth joined her tongue in tiny erotic nibbles at his nipples while her hands moved around to the small of his back to knead and massage the muscles rhythmically, delighting in the feel of his smooth skin.

She was dimly aware that her actions were building a white-hot arousal in Rafe, and it filled her with the same primitive satisfaction that she'd known last night. She loved the tensing of that massive, strong body as she touched him with her tongue or with a feather-light brush of her hair as she leaned her face close to his chest. She loved the way he shuddered and inhaled sharply at every new, unexpected touch of her hands on his body. She could hear the rapid pace of his heartbeat beneath her ear and with joyous triumph knew it was she who had caused it to thunder.

"Enough, you little devil," Rafe said hoarsely, pushing her almost desperately away from him. "I've heard it was the Indian women who were the most inventive at torturing their prisoners, and I believe it now."

She looked up at him and grinned happily. "You didn't like it?" she asked demurely, knowing very well the effect that she'd had on him. Oh yes, he'd liked it, all right.

He gazed down, and his dark eyes narrowed as they read the satisfaction on her face. "You know I did," he said tersely. "And you're just a little too pleased about it to suit me." He ripped off her jeans and the tiny bikini panties at the same time, and Janna felt suddenly very exposed and vulnerable as she lay naked before him in the soft, fragrant bed of hay. "I think I'll just puncture a little of that smug complacency, Janna."

He was calmly stripping off the rest of his clothes, and Janna looked up at him, frowning in confusion. There was no doubt that he was tremendously aroused. The physical evidence was clear not only in the hard tension of his body but in the dark blaze of his eyes in the lean, taut hungriness of his face. When he pushed her back in the hay, she had expected him to follow her down and once more send her on that passionate odyssey they'd traveled last night. She knew now that the thought had been in the back of her mind all day, and she'd subconsciously been torn between anticipation and frustration.

Despite any mental rejection and qualifications she might have had, she *wanted* Rafe's possession of her body with a passionate ferocity that she hadn't admitted even to herself. And he wanted *her*, damn it. So why was he being so painstakingly deliberate, as he removed the remainder of his clothes and folded them neatly before tossing them aside with a maddening calmness? Then, incredibly, he was picking up another blasted napkin! "What are you doing?" she squeaked indignantly.

"I have the reputation of always finishing what I start," he told her silkily as he parted her legs and slid in between them. "Didn't you know that, Janna? You're still a little damp, sweetheart." Then he proceeded to dry her with skilled thoroughness, from the bare toes to the arching apex of her thighs—so skilled and so thorough that he had her arching and moving in a feverish torment, her head moving from side to side in a restless searching that was not to be satisfied.

"Rafe!" she cried, and there was fury as well as frustration in that exclamation, which caused him to look up with a grin that had an element of tigerish enjoyment in it.

"Not yet, Janna," he said softly. "I want you as crazy for it as I am." He reached out for the plaid blanket and with a billowing motion spread it on the hay beside them. "Roll over, darling," he said as he moved from between her legs. "I wouldn't want those lovely breasts scratched by the straw."

His hands were tender as he moved her gently onto her stomach. Then he was once more between her legs and he was playing the same maddening detailed attention to the silky line of her back and buttocks as he had to her front. Somehow it was even more erotic to be unable to see what he was doing to her, she thought breathlessly, with a painful tightening of the muscles of her stomach, to feel his hands moving over her possessively and know he was gazing at her with that almost blind look of desire in the depths of those night-dark eyes. She could hear his breathing quicken above her and she knew his restraint was being strained to the limits by this love play. God, let that control break soon, she thought feverishly. She didn't think she could stand much more of this. Her hands knotted into fists as she felt his hands gently brushing the hay from her back.

"I knew the hay would mark you," Rafe said huskily, "your skin is so silky." His finger touched a spot where her lower back joined the soft swell of her buttocks. "There's a little scratch right there." Then she felt the warmth of his breath as his lips replaced his finger in a gossamer-light kiss that burned like an electric shock.

Then the waiting was over as Rafe gave a low groan that sounded like an animal in pain. His hands weren't gentle this time when he flipped her over and joined her on the blanket with two swiftly coordinated movements. His lips were voraciously hungry on hers and his hands were running up and down her back with a feverish urgency. He was uttering little smothered groans of need deep in his throat, which were echoed by Janna's own frantic moans.

She was burning up, writhing in a flame of desire so intense she felt as if she would be devoured by it if Rafe didn't give her what she needed so desperately. She didn't know which one of them initiated their union, but suddenly they were together and Janna was clutching at Rafe's shoulders, her face convulsed with savage satisfaction.

With a swift movement that caught her by surprise, Rafe rolled over and she was on top, gazing down at him with wide, inquiring eyes, his hands on her hips binding their bodies together in indescribable excitement. "I want to see your face," Rafe explained huskily as his hips started to gyrate forcefully in an upward rhythm that caused her breath to leave her. "I want to look up and see that expression and know what I'm doing to you is causing it." He reached up and cupped her breasts in his hands. "I want to be able to hold you in my hands like this."

Janna felt as if she were exploding into a million dazzling splinters of sensation, and she started to move with the same frantic urgency that was driving Rafe, meeting him with an energy and power equal to his own. Both the tempo and intensity were so blindingly extreme, it was inevitable that it also be as evanescent as an exploding star. It seemed only an incredibly short time later that they were lying locked in each other's arms, clinging trembling to each other in the aftermath of that explosion.

Rafe's arms were possessive and sheltering about her, and Janna was too languid and weary to do anything but snuggle closer into their warm strength.

Rafe's warm lips pressed an affectionate kiss on her temple that was oddly sexless after the stormy sexuality that had preceded it, and his hand gently stroked her hair back from her face. "God, that was completely mind-blowing," he said softly. "You're quite some lady, sweetheart. If you're this fantastic as a novice, I can't wait until you've had a little practice." he chuckled. "As a matter of fact, I can't wait for the practice itself."

"You'll have to," she groaned wearily, burrowing her head deeper in the curve of his shoulder. "I may never be able to move again."

"Poor baby," he crooned huskily, brushing her forehead again with his lips. "You've had quite a workout for someone so new at the game. You shouldn't be so damned delectable. Do you know that you drive me nearly crazy with wanting you?"

How could she disbelieve him, when he had the same effect on her? she thought dreamily. "Not very gallant of you to lay the blame entirely at my door," she murmured lightly, nestling still closer to him. "I seem to recall some very active participation on your part."

"Considering your lack of experience, I didn't want to do anything to discourage you," he drawled mischievously. "It might have scarred you psychologically."

Janna gave a derisive and unladylike snort, but she didn't answer. She was too languid and content to bother with badinage. They lay for a long peaceful moment, the only sound the steady drumming of the rain on the roof. Suddenly Rafe broke into a deep, amused chuckle, and Janna tilted back her head to look at his face.

Rafe's lips were twitching, and his dark eyes twinkling with mischief, as he said solemnly, "I've heard jokes about the farmer's daughter all my life." He kissed her lightly on the tip of her nose. "And now that I've had one, I believe every one of them!"

The sun was setting in a cloud of pink and lavender glory when the helicopter landed on the pad at Santine's Castle, and Janna eyed it appreciatively as Rafe lifted her down from the copter and slammed the door behind them.

"It looks like they didn't see any rain here at all," she observed casually as he took her hand and they set out for the house.

He gave her a mocking glance. "We didn't see much rain ourselves either, if you recall," he said, his lips twitching. "Though we did hear quite a bit of it."

Janna made a face at him, and he laughed softly, his hand tightening about her own. They'd spent the entire afternoon in the hayloft making love, then lazily talking, then making love again, in a passionate cycle that probably could have gone on through the night. She remembered ruefully after that first time she'd been so replete that she couldn't imagine she'd want him again so soon. Yet he'd only had to show her his own need for her to take fire. She felt a little tingle surge through her even now as she glanced down at the play of the strong muscles of his thighs under the close-fitting pants. She looked up again quickly, color staining her cheeks. Good God, for a woman who'd been a virgin only yesterday, she was turning into a regular nymphomaniac.

They were in the courtyard now, and the rosy rays of the setting sun cast a mellow glow over the beige-and-pink tiles and gave the mansion itself an aura of welcoming warmth. It looked almost homey, Janna thought contentedly. Who would have guessed two weeks ago that she would ever have thought of Santine's Castle as home?

"Janna."

Rafe had stopped by the fountain, and she looked

up at him inquiringly, noting how the light that had
mellowed everything else only served to heighten the
bold roughness of Rafe's features. Yet there was no
hardness in his eyes right now. Strange that she'd
never realized dark eyes could be so warm.

"I want to talk to you," he said softly, his expression grave.

Janna felt a tiny ripple of uneasiness run through
her that pierced the glow of mental and physical
euphoria enfolding her. She didn't want to talk, she
thought desperately. This afternoon had been a lovely
moment out of time, and all reason and practical
considerations had been suspended. She didn't want
to give that up as yet. "Why don't we wait until after
dinner?" she suggested lightly.

He shook his head stubbornly. "Now," he said,
scowling blackly. "This isn't going to be easy for me,
and I want to get it over with."

Janna looked up, her eyes wide with alarm, and
his face softened miraculously. His hand reached
out to touch the curve of her cheek caressingly.
"Don't look like that, doe eyes," he said huskily.
"You should know by now what a rough bastard I
am. I didn't mean to frighten you. I'm just feeling
damn awkward and I don't like it."

"I'm not frightened," Janna replied calmly. But
she had been frightened for a moment. How quickly
she'd become used to seeing only tenderness and
desire on Rafe's face when he looked at her. It had
actually startled her when she'd seen that flash of
hardness in his expression just now.

"Good," Rafe said, his face oddly vulnerable as he
looked down at her. "I don't want you ever to be
afraid of me, Janna." His lips curved wryly. "That's
another first for me. I think I've always fostered an
element of fear in all my relationships; it increased
my sense of power and control."

"And that's important to you?" Janna asked gently.

"Hell, yes, it's important," Rafe said sharply. "I

had enough pushing around as a kid to last me for a lifetime. No one's ever going to have the power to do that to me again. I run things now."

"You certainly do," Janna said wryly. "I don't think you need worry about anyone trying to intimidate you these days. You're very much in control, Rafe Santine."

"Am I?" Rafe asked softly, his hand tracing the curve of her lower lip. "Somehow I don't think I am. At least not with you. I've even reached the point where I don't care whether I am or not any more. That's quite a victory for you."

"Victory?" Janna's eyes clouded with distress. "I don't think I like that term. I've never wanted any victory over you, Rafe."

"I know. You're regrettably lacking in competitive spirit. You weren't even jealous of Diane, damn it." His hands fell to her shoulders, absently kneading the muscles beneath his fingers. He frowned impatiently. "Regardless of your intentions, the result is still the same. Now, be quiet until I get this out, blast it."

Janna's lips twitched in amusement before she fell obediently silent.

"I'm probably not going to do this very well," he said gruffly, his hands tightening on her shoulders as he scowled down at her. "I want you to stay with me. Not just until I go back to San Francisco, as you've agreed." He drew a deep breath and asked abruptly. "I want you to move in with me permanently." He frowned fiercely before muttering reluctantly, "Please."

If she hadn't been so startled, Janna would have been amused and touched at that last rusty entreaty. How long had it been since Rafe had asked for anything? "You want me to become your live-in mistress?" she asked bewilderedly. "Like Diane?"

"Not like Diane," he denied roughly. "It wouldn't be

like that. I never gave a damn about Diane or any of the others." He paused, as if searching for words; then: "You're *important* to me, Janna."

"It wouldn't work," she said flatly. "You know it wouldn't work, Rafe." Why did she feel this terrible aching emptiness as she uttered those words?

"How the hell do you know it wouldn't work until you try it?" he asked, giving her a little shake that was far from loverlike. "All my life I've been making ideas and situations work that everyone told me were impossible, so don't tell me we can't do this. I'll *make* it work."

"This isn't boardroom politics or taking over a company, Rafe," Janna said huskily. "We're two individuals who are as far apart as two people could be. We don't even want the same things out of life."

"We want each other," he said grimly. "And that covers a hell of a lot of territory right there."

"You've wanted a good many women before me," Janna said coolly. "Sex may be the universal panacea, but it's never been a lasting one in your case. It would hardly be wise to base any permanent relationship on a purely physical foundation."

"So help me God, if you throw that 'biological coupling' phrase at me again, I'll break your neck," he said between his teeth. "I don't deny I fully intend to enjoy that luscious body at every opportunity. Hell, I'd like to rip the clothes off you and take you right here and now, but I want more than that." For a moment there was a curiously lost, defenseless look on his face. "I ache for you," he said softly. "I want you close to me. I want to hear you laugh and watch your expressions. I feel lonely when you're not in the same room with me." He laughed mirthlessly. "God, I sound like a love-sick kid. Well, maybe I am. I haven't had any experience with the emotion, so I'm not likely to recognize the symptoms. Am I in love with you, Janna?"

She bit her lip. "How do I know?" she asked

miserably. "I've never even thought about being in love. I doubt if it's very likely, though."

For an instant she thought she saw a flash of pain in his face, before it quickly hardened. "You're probably right," he said cynically. "Neither one of us knows anything about love." His mouth twisted bitterly. "Correction. I love my work, and you love that precious grandmother of yours. Perhaps that should be enough for us."

"Perhaps it should," Janna said, her throat tight with pain. "It's more than many people have." She looked away from him, her lashes veiling her eyes. "It's more than my grandmother had. A husband who married her to be a broodmare and a farm hand, a son who was ashamed of her, and a society that rejected her." She looked up, her eyes bright with tears. "And she's more worthy of being loved than any human being I've ever known."

"She had you," Rafe said gently.

"My grandmother is almost seventy years old," Janna said. "There were a lot of years when she didn't. She thought she'd be free when she left the reservation, but she found she'd only traded one form of bondage for another."

"So you're determined not to follow her example," Rafe said harshly. "No ties, no commitments, no inconvenient emotions that will cause you to be tempted to give up even a portion of your freedom." He shook his head wonderingly. "And I thought I was hard! I'm not asking you to give up anything, for God's sake. If you want to go on with your career at the reserve, we'll work out something so you can do it. I'm not even asking you to marry me. All I'm asking is that you stay with me until the magic goes away. Is that too much?"

Janna closed her eyes at the jolt of pain that rocked her. Lord, yes, it was too much. If she didn't love Rafe now, she was so near it that it made little difference. The longer she stayed with him, the deeper that love would grow, and she knew the magic wouldn't go away for her even if it faded for Rafe. She couldn't exchange her independence for the glittering fool's gold Rafe was offering her. "I'm sorry, I just can't do it," she whispered huskily, opening eyes that were strained and haunted.

If possible, Rafe's expression became even grimmer. "You mean you won't do it," he said harshly. His hands slowly loosened their grip on her shoulders and then dropped to his sides, releasing her. "Well, I still have three weeks of your company to look forward to. It's amazing what can sometimes be accomplished in three weeks." He gestured toward the house. "Shall we go in to dinner?"

She shot him a confused sidewise glance as she turned and fell into step with him. He intercepted the look and gave her a sardonic smile. "Are you thinking that I'm surrendering too easily?" he asked mockingly. "Very perceptive of you, Janna. But then, you're a very intelligent woman." He continued to stroll toward the courtyard door, his hand grasping her elbow politely. "I still intend to get exactly what I want," he said coolly. "If you won't give, I'll have to take." He smiled bitterly. "I'm good at that. I've had a hell of a lot of practice. I should have known better than to ask you in the first place. I've never yet found that 'ask and you shall receive' maxim to be effective."

There was a thread of pain rippling beneath that bitter mockery that sent an answering hurt flooding through Janna. "You can't force me to stay with you, Rafe," she said quietly. "There's really nothing you can do."

"You're wrong," he said coolly. "There's always something that can be done, an angle to be found. I want you, Janna, perhaps more than I've ever wanted anything in my life." There was absolute certainty in his voice. "I'll find a way of getting you." The impersonal glance he gave her contrasted oddly with the passion of his words. "For instance, you might consider that, at the end of those weeks, there may be something hindering your freedom that you hadn't counted on."

"What do you mean?" Janna asked, her brow creasing in puzzlement.

"I had no idea that you were a virgin last night and would need protection," he said silkily. "Not that I could have stopped at that point anyway, and today's little romp in the hay also caught me off guard. I had every intention of protecting you from now on, but I think under the circumstances we'll leave it up to fate. I hardly think you'd be so eager to leave me if you were carrying my child."

She stared at him uncertainly. "You're bluffing," she said, biting her lip worriedly. "You wouldn't want that to happen any more than I would. You're a very possessive man, Rafe. You wouldn't be able to stand it if I called your bluff and not only left but took your baby with me."

His hand tightened on her elbow. "You're quite right. I wouldn't be able to tolerate it. You'd have to marry me. I won't have any child of mine labeled a bastard." He darted her a look as hard as a saber thrust. "Nor would I permit an abortion, Janna. You can see the dangers to your freedom would be far greater if that happened. Wouldn't it be wiser to give in now and let me take care of you?"

"You're completely unscrupulous, aren't you, Rafe?" she asked wonderingly, gazing at him with wide, hurt eyes.

"Stop looking at me like that, damn it," Rafe grated out violently. "Hell, yes, I can be ruthless, but I didn't want to be that way with you. I wanted to be gentle."

"Your good intentions didn't last long, did they?" Janna asked dully.

"No, I guess they didn't," Rafe said wearily, his expression bleak. "Perhaps I should have started with something less important to me. I'm not letting you go, Janna. Make up your mind to that. One way or another, you're going to belong to me."

She shook her head. "No, Rafe."

He opened the brass-studded courtyard door and stood aside to let her pass. "Yes, Janna," he said softly. "Definitely, yes."

Seven

The digital clock on the bedside table cast out a blue lambent glow in the darkness, but Janna didn't need to glance at it to know it was after three in the morning. She had been strenuously avoiding looking at it since she'd gone to bed five hours ago, but the flickering numerals seemed to be engraved on her lids whenever she closed her eyes. She turned restlessly in the king-sized bed, feeling lost and lonely in its huge expanse.

It had been three nights since that painful confrontation in the courtyard, and Rafe had not seen fit to share this monster of a bed or the facilities of the master suite with her in all that time. In fact, she'd scarcely seen him during the entire period. He'd left her directly after dinner that first evening and closeted himself in the library with Dawson. She didn't know where Rafe was sleeping or even if he was, for he had seldom left the library during those three days. The glimpses she had of Pat Dawson's face as he occasionally hastened from the library to his own office to get some file or other had revealed he was harried and exhausted. It was obvious that Rafe was driving them both to the point of collapse, and it made no sense at all.

After those far-from-subtle threats he had made in the courtyard, why had he suddenly abandoned his determination to coerce her into staying with him? Why was he virtually ignoring her and driving himself to exhaustion in that damned office? She supposed she should have been grateful that he had given up his plan of pressuring her, but she felt a strange unease, almost guilt, when she remembered the fleeting look of pain on Rafe's face that last afternoon.

It was just like the man to do this to her, she thought in exasperation as she twisted restlessly on the silken sheets. Why couldn't he react predictably instead of behaving with his usual arrogant stubbornness and individuality. Damn it, he had been ill, and it must have been fairly serious to incapacitate a man of Rafe's almost bull-like strength. This constant driving labor was enough to break the health of a well man, much less one who'd been ordered to rest. If Pat had looked so exhausted, what must Rafe be feeling at this moment? The irritating man would probably be back in the hospital if he kept on at this pace.

She felt a sudden chill at the thought of Rafe lying weak and still in a sterile white hospital bed, and her heart started to thump with panic. It didn't matter that the idiot probably deserved everything that happened to him. She was actually feeling physically ill with worry at that horribly vivid picture, and she felt a bead of moisture break out on her forehead. Why didn't someone stop him? Pat Dawson must know where this type of thing would lead for a man who'd been as ill as Rafe. Why didn't he tell Rafe what a fool he was to risk a setback like the one he was courting so recklessly?

She bit her lip, frowning in frustration as she realized just how ridiculous that possibility would be. Dawson was well aware that he would be no match for Rafe even if he weren't in a subservient position. At any hint of interference, Rafe could annihilate him with either that scathing tongue or the power he wielded so ruthlessly. No, she could expect no help from Pat.

She could expect no help? What was she thinking? Rafe Santine's welfare wasn't any concern of hers. It certainly wasn't her responsibility if he wanted to work himself back into a hospital bed. But if she wouldn't accept the burden of his well-being, who would? The fear and wariness that he engendered in those around him made him vulnerable to the ramifications of his own iron determination. He stood curiously alone, and Janna felt a throbbing ache as she realized the extent of that self-imposed loneliness.

She blinked furiously to rid her eyes of those maddening tears, and drew a long, shaky breath. The cowards would probably let him kill himself before they gathered enough courage to beard him in his den. Well, she couldn't stand it any longer. Someone had to tell him a few home truths, and it seemed she was elected.

Without stopping to think, she threw back the velvet coverlet and slipped naked from the bed, stopping only to grab her honey-colored satin negligee and slip it on as she strode swiftly toward the door. She hurriedly buttoned the long, flowing robe as she traversed the corridor and flew down the stairs, her bare feet padding with catlike sureness on the plush Persian-carpet runner. It was dark in the hall, but she could see the thin line of light beneath the library door as she marched almost militantly toward it.

"Miss Cannon."

The words had been almost a whisper, but, coming out of the darkened foyer behind her, caused her heart to nearly jump out of her breast. She whirled around in alarm, her startled eyes searching the darkness.

"I apologize for frightening you," Stokley said quietly, coming forward with his usual regal bearing. He was in his customary discreet black jacket and looked as serenely wide awake as if it were three in the afternoon and not the middle of the night. He was carefully carrying a tray with a silver carafe of coffee and a single cup and saucer. "I wonder if I might impose on you to take this tray in to Mr. Santine while I bring another cup and saucer for you."

Janna accepted the tray. "That won't be necessary," she said, her tone as hushed as Stokley's had been. "You can go on to bed, Fred. I only came down to persuade Mr. Santine to go to bed himself. He won't need you any more tonight."

In the shadowy dimness she couldn't discern his expression, but there was relief and approval in his voice as he answered. "I'm very glad to hear that, Miss Cannon. It wasn't my place to make the suggestion, but I'm sure Mr. Santine is overdoing it a bit. You're sure I can't be of any further service? Perhaps you might ask him if he'd like a snack before he retires. The maid said he barely touched his supper tray."

"If he decides that he wants something, I'm sure we can find our way to the kitchen, Fred," Janna said impatiently. "Run along to bed. There's no use for the entire household to be stirring just because Mr. Santine doesn't know night from day."

There was an instant of shocked silence, and when Stokley replied, there was a thread of amusement in his voice. "If you say so, Miss Cannon. May I open the door for you?"

"Yes, please," she answered absently. "Good night, Fred."

"Good night, Miss Cannon."

The silver tray and carafe were surprisingly heavy, and she kept her eyes lowered and fixed on her burden as she passed through the door, which Stokley then closed quietly behind her.

"For God's sake, stop dillydallying and put down the coffee and get out, Fred," Rafe said roughly. "I told you I didn't want it to begin with."

Janna glanced up to see just what she expected to

see. Rafe Santine was sitting hunched over the desk, in the massive leather executive chair, his gaze on the paper he was perusing in the pool of light from the desk lamp. It was the only light in the room, with the exception of the flickering blaze in the fireplace across the room. The sleeves of his crisp white shirt were rolled up to the elbow, baring brown, muscular forearms, and he'd unfastened the first few buttons for comfort, revealing the strong line of his throat. There was a dark lock of hair falling carelessly on his forehead, and the broad planes of his face were boldly prominent, the skin stretched taut with strain.

"Good," Janna said composedly, gliding forward silently to place the heavy tray on a corner of the mahogany desk. "Caffeine can't be good for you at this time of night anyway."

Rafe looked up quickly, surprise rapidly superseded by guarded cynicism as he saw her standing there watching him from the other side of the desk, her slim, graceful form in the honey satin robe shimmering in the lamplight.

"On second thought, I believe I will have a cup," he said, leaning back in his chair to regard her mockingly. "Pour me one and bring it over here, Janna."

Janna sighed impatiently, gritting her teeth in exasperation as she picked up the carafe and poured the hot black brew into the cup. It was obvious Rafe was in one of his more difficult moods, reacting like a stubborn little boy to any hint of coercion. She looked up to see his brooding eyes fixed on her hands as she picked up the cup and saucer. "You do that quite beautifully," he said absently. "There's something intrinsically serene and graceful about the action, almost a homeliness." He looked up to smile mirthlessly. "It's very deceptive, for there's no one less domestic or home-oriented than you. Isn't that right, my little wild thing?"

She didn't answer as she came around the desk to place the coffee before him on the desk. She would have stepped back, but he stopped her, his hand swiftly grasping her wrist. "No, stay," he ordered curtly, his lips curving sardonically. "I want to have something pretty to look at while I enjoy my coffee."

She shrugged, and half sat, half leaned on the corner of the desk, watching him as he picked up the cup and took a sip, his hand still loosely holding her wrist. "That coffee is awfully strong," she said, frowning disapprovingly. "It's going to make it difficult for you to sleep."

"Your concern is touching," he drawled caustically, taking another swallow. "Is that why you decided to honor me with your presence? Are you playing little mother?" His lips curled scornfully. "You'll forgive me if I lack appreciation for the nuances of the role. I'm afraid my childhood was lacking in the gentle maternal influences." He shrugged. "It's just as well; I never really needed it." He took another drink of coffee, his eyes fixed challengingly on her face. "I still don't."

He was so much like a difficult little boy issuing a dare to all comers that she felt a queer tug at her heart. She carefully smothered a smile of amusement. "I agree," she said briskly. "You've absolutely no need for a mother. But you could use the services of a game warden, and I'm uniquely qualified in that area. I'm used to dealing with stubborn, irascible beasts."

His eyes widened in surprise, and there was a blank instant of silence before he gave a short bark of laughter. His gaze narrowed on her face. "I'm waiting with bated breath for you to tell me just what sort of beast you think you've caught in your magic spell, Pocahontas," he said silkily.

She cocked her head consideringly, studying him objectively. "Well, your roar is rather like a lion's, you have the bad temper of a rhinoceros, and the callous toughness of an elephant," she said gently. "I think that about covers it."

"At least you didn't draw any mental comparisons with your animal friends," Rafe said wryly. "I suppose I should be grateful for small favors."

"I was coming to that," Janna said. "I just wanted to get the more obvious similarities out of the way first. Actually, in that department you rival the dodo bird, which is probably why it's extinct. Is there some reason why you're trying to follow its example?"

"Perhaps I'm trying to arouse your sympathy," he answered, scowling. "It appears that only an endangered species can lay claim to your long-term interest."

She flinched. "You'll make that list in short order if you don't take better care of yourself," she retorted tartly. "You're supposed to be convalescing. Do you want to kill yourself?"

"Bull!" he shot back gruffly, crashing the cup down in the saucer with barely restrained violence. "I'm almost well. A few late sessions at my desk won't hurt me."

"You know very well your doctor forbade any concentrated work schedule," Janna said fiercely. "You've been slaving like a maniac for the past three days. Even Pat is beginning to look exhausted."

"Pat?" Rafe asked, his voice tight, his dark eyes flaring. "I should have known it wasn't any concern for me that caused your nocturnal visit. Did Dawson come running to you for sympathy? I'm sure he was willing to accept all that sentimental maternal balderdash you're offering." His hand tightened agonizingly about her wrist. "And a good deal more." His face grew taut, and his eyes narrowed menacingly. "What else did you offer him, Janna?"

"Nothing," Janna gasped, struggling vainly to release herself from his clasp. "For God's sake, he's practically been in your back pocket for days. When would I get the chance to vamp the poor man? Will you please let me go? You're hurting me."

"I want to hurt you," he said harshly, and, incredibly, she felt his hand tighten on her wrist with bruising ferocity. She gave an involuntary cry as a white-hot jolt of pain ripped through her, and he dropped her wrist as if he'd been burned.

She stared dazedly at her wrist, which was white with livid streaks from the pressure he'd exerted in that sudden brutal clasp. Instinctively she reached out her other hand to cover the marks, as if they were a brand of shame.

"You can't hide them," Rafe said dully, his eyes fixed on her arm in almost morbid fascination. "You'll probably be bruised black and blue tomorrow." He lifted his head, and his eyes were so sick and tormented that Janna felt her breath catch in her throat. "I really am the beast you named me."

"No," Janna said quickly, pulling the long, loose sleeve of the negligee over her wrist. "It was an accident. You really didn't mean to hurt me."

"Didn't I?" he asked bitterly. "I think I did." He shook his head slowly, his face white and set. "I think I wanted you to feel something, anything, even if it was pain or hatred for me. I couldn't stand being the only one in this quagmire of emotion. Do you think I didn't know it was only pity that caused you to come to me tonight? You stand there looking so damn beautiful that it makes me ache inside, and I want to explode and strike out at everything in sight." He smiled bitterly. "Well, I did strike out, didn't I?" He closed his eyes. "God, I feel sick."

"You're exhausted," Janna said. That look of pain and supreme self-disgust was hurting her far more than Rafe's temporary loss of control. "If you'd been yourself, I know you'd never have touched me."

He leaned forward and buried his face in his hands. "Oh, I would have touched you." He laughed mirthlessly. "Perhaps not in violence, but I assure you that I'd have touched you. Why do you think I've been working myself into a frazzle since we got back from the reserve?"

"I don't understand," she said falteringly, wishing desperately he would once more assume that hard, ruthless mask with which he usually faced the world. This vulnerable, pain-wracked Rafe slipped effortlessly beneath the barriers she had lifted.

He raised his head and opened his eyes. "I didn't expect you to," he said wearily. "I'm well aware I'm all alone in this. Let's just say it's my last-ditch struggle against this damn spell you've woven about me. My work has always been the most fascinating mistress I've known. No other woman has ever stood a chance against it. I thought if I could drown myself in it, I could forget you."

"And did you?" Janna asked softly.

"Well, it made me so tired that it kept me out of your bed," he answered bitterly. "But it didn't keep me from thinking about you or wanting you. I don't know why I thought it would work. Nothing else has." His sable gaze was suddenly flaring with anger. "And now I've hurt you, damn it! Why couldn't you stay away from me? Didn't your precious training ever teach you to stay away from an animal in pain?"

"No," Janna said quietly. "It taught me to try to remove the source of the pain and heal the hurt." She stepped forward and gently brushed the errant lock of hair from his forehead. "Why won't you believe that you didn't really hurt me?" He went suddenly still as her hand soothingly stroked his dark, glossy hair. "I'll probably not even have a bruise tomorrow." Her voice was laced with humor as she continued. "I'm accustomed to far worse casualties every day at the reserve."

He reached out and carefully took her other hand in his and pushed up the loose satin sleeve to reveal the livid brand. "Nice try," he said tautly, staring at the already darkening flesh with compulsive fascination. "But you'll carry those marks for days. I've been in enough barroom brawls to know that."

She didn't try to remove her hand from his, but her other hand continued its soothing stroking motion in the silky darkness of his hair. "Then you must know these look much worse then they are," she replied quietly. "I bruise very easily."

"I think you're lying to me," he said gruffly, his thumb rubbing the marks with infinite gentleness, as if trying to erase the discoloration. "I don't imagine you'll try removing the thorn from this particular lion's paw again anytime soon." He suddenly raised her wrist and passionately pressed his lips to it. "God, I'm sorry." His voice was husky. He pulled her swiftly into the circle of his arms and buried his face in her breast like a repentant little boy. "I must have gone a little crazy. I won't do it again. I promise."

"I know you won't," Janna said gently, holding his head to her softness with a fierce possessiveness she'd never known before. "I know it won't happen again."

"You smell so sweet," he whispered, his arms tightening around her. "The scent of you makes me dizzy."

"It's probably exhaustion causing that effect," Janna said lightly, over the lump in her throat. "I doubt if lavender bath salts could prove quite so potent."

"Is that what it is?" he asked absently, rubbing his cheek in sensual contentment against the satin material of her negligee. "It does smell a little like flowers. But there's something else that's just you. It's sweet clover and fresh sea breeze and warm, fragrant woman." He hugged her closer still. "I like it."

Janna was breathless from more than the tightness of his embrace. The warmth of his lips through the thin satin was causing her heart to accelerate in quantum leaps. She'd made an amazingly simple transition from moving empathy to a hot, aching desire to take as well as give a more physical comfort. She made an involuntary motion of withdrawal as she realized that Rafe's virile masculinity was making her forget the original reason she'd come to him.

"No," he said thickly, his arms defeating the movement at its inception. "Don't leave me. I'm not going to hurt you again. I just want you close to me."

He pulled her down into his lap and pressed her head into the hollow of his shoulder. The oxford cloth of his shirt, crisp and warm from his body heat, was against her cheek, and she could discern the shadowy darkness of the thick wiry hair of his chest beneath its pristine whiteness. "This isn't right," she protested faintly. "You should go to bed and rest."

"Well, part of your plan has appeal," Rafe said softly, his lips brushing her temple gently. "But I don't think I can wait for even that formality."

Cradling her in his arms, his hands were deft as he swiftly loosened her braid, running his fingers through the tresses until they were falling in unruly, shimmering profusion about her shoulders. His hands wound passionately in her hair as he tilted her head to look into her eyes. "I want you," he said thickly. "Will you let me make love to you, Janna?"

Her lashes lowered to veil her eyes. "I thought you'd made it clear I was to have no choice on that score," she answered. "If I remember, you were quite adamant about your rights and privileges for the next few weeks."

He flinched, and his hands tightened painfully in her hair. "Do you think I wanted to threaten you like that?" he asked. "You left me no option."

"Yet tonight you're giving me one," she pointed out. "Have you had second thoughts?"

He scowled darkly. "Damn it, do you have to be so blasted analytic? Can't you just say yes or no?" Then, as she didn't answer, he sighed resignedly. "No, I haven't changed my mind," he growled. "If I've learned

anything in these past few days, it's that if you're a
thorn in my flesh, it's a thorn I can't do without. I'll
keep you any way I can." His eyes were moody, and
his manner a little awkward. "I won't lie to you,
Janna. I'll probably use every ploy and subterfuge I
can think of to make sure you stay with me, but
tonight I want you to come to me willingly." He
picked up her wrist and once again pressed his lips
to the bruised flesh. "I won't use force or coercion
on you." His lips twisted wryly. "You have no idea
just how heroic a sacrifice that entails."

"If I choose, you'll let me get up and walk out that
door?" Janna asked, not looking at him.

His body stiffened. "I will," he said slowly.

She straightened slowly, so that she was upright
in his lap. His hands fell reluctantly away from her
hair, and she smoothed it composedly before she
stood up and moved a few paces away. She turned
to face him. "But I don't want to walk out that
door," Janna said, smiling serenely. "I want you to
make love to me. You're a very exciting lover, Rafe. If
you're so determined in your course of action, why
shouldn't I enjoy its more pleasant aspects?" Her
lips quirked. "Besides, it may be the only way I can
get you to go to bed."

"Bed, hell," Santine growled. He was on his feet in
seconds and across the yard or so separating them.
"I've been on the verge of raping you since I looked
up and saw you shimmering in the lamplight like a
sexy ghost." Then she was in his arms and he was
covering her face and throat with quick, scorching
kisses. "Since this seems to be my only talent that
appeals to you, I'll be damned if I'll wait any longer
to demonstrate it." Despite the roughness of his
words, his large hands were exquisitely gentle as
they traveled up to cup the fullness of her breasts.
"We made out pretty well in a hayloft. That couch
should be sheer luxury in comparison." He nodded
toward the conversation area on the far side of the

room, and his lips brushed hers in a kiss of lingering sweetness. "I promise you won't be uncomfortable. I want to show you I'm not always a rough, undisciplined bastard," he muttered. "I want to be gentle with you, sweetheart."

And he *was* gentle as he picked her up and carried her to the wide russet morocco leather couch before the fireplace. He was even more gentle as he lay her on its cushioned softness, sat down beside her, and slowly unbuttoned the satin negligee. His expression was intent and beautifully sensual as he carefully opened the honey-colored folds and gazed down at her with an intense hunger that caused a tingle of electricity to shoot through her. His large, blunt hands were gentle, too, as they moved over her sleek midriff in a caress all the more erotic for its teasing lightness. And when his raven-dark head bent, his tongue brushing one aroused nipple with warm, soft slowness, that, too, was done with infinite gentleness.

The only element lacking in gentleness was the flickering violence in the depths of Rafe's eyes and the charged tension of the powerful muscles of his body as he fought for the restraint he'd promised her. Somehow, the knowledge of that passionate, leashed violence gave the slow softness of his caresses a dark, hot sensuality that was almost unbearably exciting.

He straightened slowly, and drew a deep, ragged breath, his hands quickly unbuttoning his white shirt, while his gaze remained on Janna's dreamy, languid face. "God, it seems like weeks instead of days since I've seen you like this," he said huskily as he slipped out of the shirt and threw it carelessly on the red and cream of the Persian carpet. The rest of his clothes swiftly followed. "Do you know how you look with the firelight playing over that lovely naked body? You're all flame and dusky rose and sweet, deep shadows."

"You're beautiful, too," Janna said dreamily, reaching out with both hands to touch the thick dark mat of hair on his chest. At his snort of disbelief she protested sincerely. "You *are* beautiful. Oh, perhaps you're not a classical Adonis or a Robert Redford, but there's more to beauty than that. Your body is truly magnificent, and your face . . ." She hesitated, trying to put into words the force and fascination of that rough, almost brutally powerful countenance. "It has expressions and strength and—"

She broke off as he leaned forward to press a swift, hard kiss on her lips. "Will you please be still and let me love you?" he said hoarsely as his hands slowly closed on her breasts, his thumbs moving in an abrasive stroking motion across her nipples and sending a streak of fire through her. "I'm holding on to my self-control by the skin of my teeth at the moment." His hands moved down to rub the softness of her belly, and his warm, intent gaze followed the motion of his hands with narrowed eyes. His voice was deep and smoky as he continued, almost to himself, "You know, you were right. I am rather like an animal, but not the ones you compared me to."

"What?" Janna asked dazedly. The molten languid heat building in her loins was being stoked with every lazy motion of his hands. "You know that I was joking."

"Perhaps you hit closer to the truth than you knew," he said softly, his hands parting her legs to stroke the inside of her thighs with a light, tantalizing brush of his fingertips that caused her to inhale sharply. "I've always been proud of my strength and invulnerability. I was king of the forest, indomitable and unattainable." He was stroking at the very heart of her now, and she heard his words through a heated haze. "Do you know the story of the unicorn and the maiden?" He didn't wait for an answer, which was fortunate, for she couldn't have replied anyway. "The unicorn was a mythical animal who had that same strength and indomitability, yet the hunters who pursued him for his golden horn found he had one fatal weakness. They had only to set a young virgin in a forest clearing and the unicorn would be drawn to her as if by magic, and would kneel and place his head in her lap." He lifted his eyes to meet her own with an intensity that pierced the sensual haze that he was creating with the magic movement of his hands. "Then the hunters could fall upon him and bind him with their golden ropes and use him as they would. The legend never says what happened to the maiden. Presumably she strolled away as cool and uncaring as before she enticed him into her spell." His smile was bitter-sweet and caused a queer ache to tighten her throat. "Do you recognize the parallels, lovely maiden?"

Without taking his eyes from her face, he deliberately lowered his head and placed it on the softness of her belly, the thick, anthracite darkness of his crisp hair nestling back and forth upon her satin smoothness like the sensual creature of his story. "Will you take your unicorn home, or turn him over to the hunters and walk away, Janna?"

For a moment she couldn't answer. Her doe-brown eyes were shining with unshed tears, and she experienced an almost primitive desire to clutch that dark head to her with a passionate fierceness. It was the most poignant emotional moment she had ever known, and suddenly she couldn't bear it. She had to break that fragile intensity or she felt she would shatter herself, like a piece of fine Venetian crystal.

Her hand reached down and caressed the hard contours of his cheek. "Your parallels aren't exactly precise," she said huskily. "It's you who are binding me with the ropes of gold. I'm not a virgin." Her eyes twinkled. "And I have no intention of letting the hunters have your horn. I have use for it myself."

For an instant there was a flicker of disappointment in the depths of his eyes. Then he again gave her that peculiarly bittersweet smile. "And so do I, sweetheart," he said lightly, and he came over her, with surprising grace for such a massive man. "How stupid of me to forget the order of our priorities. I'll try not to be so tritely sentimental again."

"Rafe . . ." Janna protested, biting her lip. "I didn't mean—"

"I know exactly what you meant," Rafe said, his lips curving in a mocking smile, as he came between her parted thighs in a surging motion that took away her breath and split the universe into a million shimmering suns. "I won't disappoint you, Janna. I'll give you what you want from me."

He was true to his word. Yet when the final climactic explosion came and they were clinging desperately to each other, their hearts thundering with the physical response as violent as the emotional one that had gone before, his sandpaper-velvet voice was a somber murmur in her ear.

"Poor unicorn . . ."

Eight

"Who the hell is Jody?" Rafe asked grimly, dark eyes blazing, as he strode into the library and slammed the door behind him.

Janna looked up, startled, as she replaced the telephone receiver and sat up straight in the massive desk chair. "I didn't know you were there, Rafe," she said quietly.

"Obviously," Rafe said caustically. "Otherwise I wouldn't have heard you crooning so confidentially to another man."

Janna leaned back in the chair and regarded him wearily. She wasn't up to facing this at the moment. As always, she felt drained after talking to Jody, and she was more upset than usual, after the report he'd given her. "Jody Forrester," she replied, gazing blindly down at the green blotter on the desk before her. "He manages the farm for my grandmother."

"The scrap of conversation I overheard hardly sounded very businesslike," Rafe said tightly. "I'd say you know each other very well."

She couldn't remember what she'd said to Jody. It couldn't have been very intimate; she'd been too upset. But it wouldn't take much to set off Rafe's burning jealousy. He'd been completely unreasonable in the two weeks since that night in the study. "We're very good friends," she agreed cautiously. "We grew up together and attended the same university."

"Very good friends." He spoke between clenched

teeth. He was striding toward her with the menacing grace of a stalking panther. "You told him you'd
talk to him again tomorrow. I should have guessed
even the most devoted granddaughter would hardly
find it necessary to call her relative long distance
every three days unless there was another attraction."
He had reached her chair and, grasping her by the
shoulders, he jerked her to her feet. "Now it appears
you plan on having your little chats daily."

"You don't understand," she faltered, her eyes brimming with tears. "It's nothing like you're imagining.
Jody is—"

"I don't want to hear anything more about your
Jody," he interrupted harshly. "And I don't want
you hearing from him either. The phone calls with
him have to stop."

"No!" Her voice was sharp, and she instinctively
moved to escape his hold in an unconscious act
of rejection. "These phone calls were part of our
agreement."

"I agreed that you could call your grandmother,
not some old college sweetheart," he snarled, tightening his hands on her shoulders. "You're the one
who's reneging on our agreement. Isn't Dawson
enough to keep you amused?"

"I barely speak to Pat. You've seen to that," Janna
cried, goaded out of her apathy. "I'm afraid for the
man's job if I so much as ask him to pass the salt.
You've been utterly impossible for days."

"But not at night, Janna," he taunted, his lips
twisting bitterly. "You always forgive me my churlish-
ness in public as long as I can give you what you need
in the bedroom. Isn't that true?"

"No, it's not true," Janna said desperately, her
brown eyes flashing. "I don't forgive you. You're making both of our lives hell, and it doesn't make any
sense. These last two weeks should convince you
better than any argument from me how miserable
we'd both be if I decided to stay with you."

"It wouldn't be like this," Rafe insisted moodily, looking down at her. "I know I've been difficult lately, but it's only because I'm not sure of you. If I knew you were mine, I wouldn't have this jealousy tearing at my insides all the time," he finished haltingly. "I'd be good to you, Janna."

"By forbidding me to call my grandmother?" Janna asked caustically. She tore herself from his grip and backed a few steps away from him. "We haven't even been able to talk to each other lately, Rafe. If I'd felt I could have confided in you, I would have told you about Jody. I would have told you everything. But how do you expect me to get past that cast-iron wall of suspicion that you've built around yourself?"

Rafe's dark eyes flickered with an emotion that might have been pain, but Janna was too upset to notice anyone's torment but her own at that moment. She shrugged helplessly. "Oh, what's the use?" she finished miserably.

She turned and almost ran from the library, ignoring the imperious calling of her name. She instinctively headed for the courtyard door, and it was only when the house was far behind her that she slowed her pace through the woods and lost a little of the nagging sensation of being under surveillance. Even that was probably deceptive, she thought bitterly. One of Rafe's security men was probably observing her right now, courtesy of those blasted video cameras planted about the estate. Well, at least that observation was impersonal. It had none of the brooding suspicion and black jealousy Rafe himself was displaying of late.

The period had been one of almost unbearable tension for everyone at the Castle, with Rafe snarling at everyone like an animal in torment. Janna shied instinctively away from the simile and tried to forget the hint of pain she could occasionally detect beneath the darkness of his anger. She mustn't soften or she'd be lost. She desperately needed Rafe's arms around her right now, and she was almost willing to buy that comfort at any price he demanded.

It wasn't exactly what Jody had said but the hesitancy and evasions dotting their conversation today that had upset her. It was almost over. The knowledge was stark and clear, shining like a smooth, polished stone at the bottom of a pool rippled by distortions. How long would it be now? she wondered desperately.

She had reached the headlands of the cliff, but she was too restless to sit tamely in the gazebo, as was her custom. Instead she took the rough, steep path leading down to the beach. And she walked.

It was almost sundown when she felt sufficiently calm to return to the house. The stormy crashing of the waves against the rocks was strangely soothing to the turbulence of her own spirit, and it was with reluctance that she slowly retraced her path to the Castle.

As she left the perimeter of the woods, she was startled to hear the purr of an automobile coming up the long, curving driveway from the gatehouse at the bottom of the hill. As far as she knew, Rafe wasn't expecting any visitors this evening, but the white Mercedes approaching would never have gotten in if Rafe hadn't agreed. Impulsively she turned away from the path leading to the courtyard and walked briskly toward the front entrance.

As she turned the corner of the house, the white Mercedes pulled to a swishing halt. Almost on cue, the front door opened and Rafe sauntered down the three shallow steps to the driveway. The Mercedes door swung open, and two long, luscious legs emerged, followed immediately by an equally luscious body, garbed in a simple little white dress that was obviously haute couture.

"Rafe, darling," the woman caroled, giving him a dazzling smile. "I was on my way to San Francisco to visit the Pembrooks and I couldn't resist stopping by to see you." She stood on tiptoe to give him a lingering kiss on the lips. "It's been a long time," she breathed softly, her violet eyes glowing like stars in the madonnalike perfection of her face. Even the woman's silky ebony hair enhanced the madonna look, pulled back simply in a chignon to better reveal those lovely classical features.

"Not so long, Marina," Rafe said coolly, returning the kiss with a casual familiarity. "Paris, four months ago, wasn't it?"

"At least you remember that." The woman pouted. "You didn't remember to call me, as you promised, once you'd returned to the States."

"I doubt if you missed me for long, Marina," Rafe drawled cynically. "The last I heard, you were being kept very well occupied by some tennis pro or other."

"He was amusing, but he wasn't you, Rafe," the woman said softly, her violet eyes glowing. "None of them are you. I would have followed you to San Francisco if I hadn't heard Diane Simmons was receiving all your attention these days. Imagine my surprise when I ran into Diane at a party in Los Angeles last week."

"Surprise? I'm sure you were aware our little affair could hardly be termed a deathless passion," he drawled. "It was more—" Suddenly he broke off, as he caught sight of Janna, hesitating several yards away. His expression of relief was quickly superseded by an impatient frown. "You've been gone for hours. Where the hell have you been?" he asked, ignoring the dark beauty on his arm as if she didn't exist. "I was about to call out security. Did it ever occur to you to let anyone know where you're going?"

Janna could feel the color flood her cheeks as she met the slightly amused smile of the other woman. "I was down on the beach," she said curtly, glaring back at him. "I didn't think it was necessary to ask permission to take a walk." Her chin lifted defiantly as she strode forward. "Now, if you'll excuse me, I think it's time I dressed for dinner." She would have brushed disdainfully by the two on the steps if Rafe hadn't caught her by the arm.

"In a moment," Rafe said silkily. "But first let me introduce you to our guest." He slipped a firm arm about her waist to keep her from escaping. "Janna, this is the Countess Marina D'Agliano, a very old friend." His lips twisted mockingly. "I'm sure Diane told you all about Janna Cannon, Marina."

"She did mention her, of course," Marina D'Agliano said coolly, her eyes running patronizingly over Janna's tousled hair and jean-clad figure. "You're not quite what I expected, Miss Cannon."

She must look like a scruffy tomboy compared to Rafe's other women, Janna thought gloomily. It was no wonder this raving beauty was gazing at her so quizzically. "How do you do, Countess D'Agliano?" she said quietly. "I'm very happy to meet you." She shrugged away from Rafe's hold. "Now, as you can tell, I really must change. I trust that I'll see you at dinner?"

"If I'm invited," the countess drawled softly, fluttering her long lashes alluringly.

"Naturally you're invited," Rafe said tersely, his eyes following Janna as she climbed the steps and opened the front door. "You'll stay the night, too, of course. I'll have Stokley show you to a guest room."

Janna closed the door behind her with a sigh of relief, and then strode across the foyer and quickly mounted the stairs. She'd thought the situation couldn't get any worse, but it seemed she was wrong. God knows, she could have done without that exquisite nymphomaniac hanging on Rafe all evening. From what she'd overheard it was clear the countess was one of Rafe's ex-mistresses, eager to regain her place in his bed. Dammit, why couldn't she have waited another week before she put in her appearance? It was going to be painful enough leaving

Rafe, without being forced to view possible successors at these agonizingly close quarters.

Forty-five minutes later, she was gazing critically at herself in the full-length mirror in the master bedroom. The velvet gown exactly the delicate shade found inside a seashell, was deliciously becoming to her dark complexion and rich brown hair. Its tiny cap sleeves and low round neck beautifully displayed her bare arms and the tempting fullness of her breasts, but the empire waistline and elegant straight lines of the skirt lent her a regal dignity. Without thinking she quickly stroked on lipstick the exact shade of the gown and a trace of mauve eyeshadow, which deepened the sparkle of her eyes. She briefly considered unbraiding her hair and arranging it in a more sophisticated style, when she remembered Rafe's murmured remark as he'd unbraided it that first night they'd spent together. No, she'd leave it just as it was despite the silken worldliness of the countess's coiffure. She was reaching for the pink velvet shawl that matched the gown when the impact of her own actions came home to her with stunning force.

She was instinctively competing for Rafe's attention as if she were some eager little harem girl anxious to guard her lord's favor from possible rivals! It had taken only the arrival of Rafe's ex-mistress on the scene to cause this loss of dignity and independence. My God, what if he'd actually decided to replace her? What lengths would she have gone to in order to retain the passion that had been hers for such a short time? She hadn't even been aware what deep inroads Rafe had made on her independence, until this sickening moment of revelation. Good God, another month with him and she'd be as much of a puppet in his hands as Diane Simmons had been!

No! She strode swiftly into the adjoining bath, her hands working swiftly at the fastening of the braid.

Ten minutes later she gazed with fierce satisfaction at the cloud of burnished brown hair that hung in a straight and shining mass about her shoulders. Then, without giving herself a chance to think, she tossed the brush on the vanity and strode swiftly out of the bathroom.

Pat Dawson was the sole occupant of the living room when she entered a few moments later, and he swiftly rose to his feet with the smiling courtesy she'd come to expect from him. His gaze ran over her with frank appreciation. "Lovely," he announced, sauntering across the room to the bar. "Your usual tomato juice?"

"Yes, thank you," Janna said quietly, following him across the room and perching on the black moroccan leather barstool. "Where's Rafe?"

Pat nodded toward the French doors. "The lovely countess decided that she wanted to take a walk before dinner." He grimaced mockingly. "Lord knows why. It's damn chilly out there, now that the sun has gone down, and she certainly doesn't appear to be the athletic type."

"Perhaps she was feeling a bit stiff from the trip," Janna suggested calmly, not meeting his eyes. She accepted the frosted glass he handed her and took a sip of the tangy liquid.

"Perhaps," Pat drawled cynically as he poured a whiskey for himself. He gazed at her thoughtfully over the rim of his glass, leaning his elbows on the bar. "You know, you're a very classy lady, Janna. I doubt if many women in your position would be as generous. You know who she is, of course?"

"Of course," Janna replied quietly, looking up to meet his concerned expression with a determined smile. "The countess isn't exactly subtle." She took another sip of her drink. "Rafe may do as he wishes. There are no ties of any sort in our relationship."

Pat shook his head ruefully. "You wouldn't have said that if you'd seen Rafe this afternoon when he wasn't able to find you. He couldn't have ranted or raved more if a takeover of AT&T had fallen through." He was turning his glass idly in his hands, his eyes fixed on the amber liquid. "And it's obvious that he's jealous as hell of you. It hasn't made these last weeks any easier for my humble self."

Janna dropped her eyes to her glass. "I'm sorry things have been difficult for you, Pat," she apologized softly. "In another week it will all be over. You and Rafe will be going back to San Francisco, and I'll start my work at the new reserve."

Pat shrugged. "It hasn't been all that bad," he said lightly. He reached out and caressingly touched a lock of her silky hair. "I've never seen you wear your hair loose before. It's very beautiful."

The closing of the French doors had the menacing incisiveness of the cocking of a pistol. The look of dark, flaming fury Janna encountered when she glanced over at Rafe, who had just entered from the terrace with Marina, was equally dangerous.

Marina D'Agliano was removing Rafe's jacket from about her shoulders and handing it to him with a dazzling smile. "Thank you, darling," she said sweetly. "I would have frozen out there without it. You know how sensitive I am to cold."

Rafe accepted the jacket without comment, shrugging into it with the leashed militancy of a condottiere donning armor, his eyes still fixed on Janna, across the room.

The countess was sweeping gracefully toward them. "Fix me a Scotch, will you, Pat?" she asked, shivering delicately. "I need something to warm me. It's so much cooler here than on the Riviera."

"Right away," he said laconically, reaching for the crystal decanter. "Anything for you, Mr. Santine?"

"No," Rafe said curtly. He had followed Marina D'Agliano and was now standing at Janna's elbow. "You've unbraided your hair," he said accusingly.

Janna nodded, looking down at her juice. "I felt the need for a change," she said briefly.

"It's gorgeous, isn't it?" Dawson asked, handing the countess her drink. "She should really wear it that way more often."

"No!" Rafe's rejection was so sharp that both Dawon and Marina D'Agliano looked at him in surprise. "I like it better braided."

The countess smoothed her own sleek chignon with one graceful hand. "How ungallant of you, Rafe. Miss Cannon looks quite sweet," she said softly, with a tinge of smug satisfaction on her face. "But then, I recall you always did prefer sophistication to girlishness."

Janna looked up calmly to meet Rafe's furious gaze. "It's regrettable that you don't like it," she said, lifting her chin defiantly. "I may decide to wear it loose permanently."

"The hell you will," Rafe muttered savagely. He drew a deep, steadying breath as he observed the shocked confusion on the faces of Dawson and the countess, and he made an obvious effort to regain his composure. "I think I'll take that drink after all, Pat," he said abruptly. "Make it a bourbon—a double."

From that point on the evening proceeded to disintegrate with predictable rapidity. During dinner Rafe was so surly and moody that even the beautiful Marina was discouraged and turned her charm on Pat Dawson. Janna's only desire was to get through this nightmare of an evening without a public confrontation with Rafe. That a private one would be forthcoming was more than clear from the way he kept staring at her from the head of the table, his gaze returning again and again to her hair with baleful animosity.

Evidently he had no intention of waiting for the end of the evening. They'd no sooner returned to the living room, and Stokley was beginning to serve the coffee, when Rafe strode to the chair where Janna was sitting and pulled her to her feet.

"You'll have to excuse Janna and me for a moment," he said tersely, his hand on her elbow. He propelled her toward the French doors. "We have something to discuss."

"But it's cold out there, Rafe," Marina protested hurriedly. "Surely your conversation could wait."

"We won't be long," Rafe said determinedly as he opened the door. "And Janna has a shawl."

The door closed behind them, but Rafe didn't pause. He half pushed, half pulled her with him across the terrace and down the stairs leading to the formal gardens. It wasn't until they were some distance from the house that he stopped and whirled to face her, his hands closing forcefully on her shoulders. There was a full moon, and the fierceness of Rafe's expression could be clearly discerned.

"Why, damn it?" he asked harshly, giving her a little shake. "Why, Janna?"

She didn't pretend to misunderstand him. "Aren't you overreacting?" she asked coolly. "It's just a hairstyle."

"It's more than that, and you know it," he said bluntly. "That belonged to me. That part of you was *mine*, damn it."

"You're wrong, Rafe," she said. "There's no part of me that belongs to anyone but myself." She stared at him defiantly. "Just as no part of you belongs to me—as the Countess D'Agliano would doubtless agree."

"I knew you'd throw Marina in my face," he said roughly. "She has nothing to do with this. I didn't invite her here, and you're the only woman I want in my bed tonight. This concerns no one but ourselves." His hands left her shoulders and buried themselves in her hair, tilting her head back to look into her face. His own face was pale and haggard in the moonlight. "Sometimes I think you're trying to drive me crazy. You knew how I'd react to this." He tugged her hair painfully. "You just wanted to see me writhing at the stake. I hope you enjoyed it, Janna. I could have killed Dawson tonight when I came in and saw him playing with your hair. I could kill you right now for letting him."

"Sometimes I wish you would," she burst out passionately. "Anything would be better than living like this." Suddenly the tears were running down her face. "I can't stand this any more, Rafe."

"Do you think I can?" he asked. "In a week you're going to walk out of my life without a backward glance." His lips twisted bitterly. "Do you know that I've started to count the days? God, how the mighty have fallen!"

The self-disgust in his voice hurt her unbearably. Without a backward glance? She would be looking over her shoulder at these weeks with Rafe for the rest of her life. "You probably won't miss me for very long," she said huskily. "You already have a replacement waiting in the wings. The countess will be more than happy to comfort you."

A swift flame of anger lit his eyes. "Damn, you're hard," he said bitterly. His hands dropped from her hair, and he stepped back. "Perhaps you're right. Maybe I haven't tried hard enough to rid myself of this obsession. There are other women in the world. Why shouldn't I let Marina practice what she does best? As I recall, she can be damn amusing." His face was stormy. "For that matter, why should I wait until you leave, to begin the cure? Tonight is as good as any other night." He whirled and strode swiftly back to the house.

Janna gazed after him, not even noticing the tears still running down her cheeks. She felt almost numb with despair, and she welcomed the numbness gladly. The pain would come soon enough. Without thinking, she turned in the opposite direction from the house and hurried through the garden to the woods beyond.

There was no way she could return to the living room and watch Marina and Rafe together. She wouldn't be able to bear being a spectator even to the opening moves of the sexual minuet between them.

She didn't know how much later it was when she found herself wandering aimlessly on the beach. The waves struck the rocks, spraying her with a fine mist that clung clammily to her skin and dampened the pink velvet dress. Somewhere she'd kicked off her high-heeled sandals, and the sand felt cold and grainy beneath her bare feet. It must have been hours, she thought wearily, for the moon was considerably lower than when Rafe and she had quarreled in the garden.

She slowly climbed the winding path to the top of the cliff, feeling oddly lethargic. She hesitated at the top, then instinctively turned away from the path that led to the castle, and moved toward the gazebo.

She was vaguely conscious of feeling an icy chill, but she couldn't determine whether it was physical or emotional. She curled up wearily on the cushions on the bench of the gazebo, wishing dazedly that she had her pink shawl to use as a cover. She must have dropped it somewhere on the beach. Well, it didn't really matter. The cold was vaguely comforting, in a strange way. At least it gave her something to think about besides Rafe and Marina D'Agliano. She felt a poignant jolt of pain and quickly blocked out the thought. She mustn't think of anything, she thought drowsily. If she didn't think, then there would be no pain. It was all very simple. So simple.

"My God!"

The fervent imprecation was breathed in Rafe's rough, sandpaper voice, and Janna felt a stirring of unease. He was angry again. He was always angry now. Then she was being carried, crushed against Rafe's solid chest, her face buried in the rough wool of his fisherman's sweater. There was something wrong about that, she thought vaguely, remembering the dark suit he'd worn at dinner. But the clean male scent was undeniably Rafe's, as was the strength of the arms that enfolded her. The voice was Rafe's, too, muttering disjointed curses against the top of her head as he strode swiftly through the woods. Anger.

"Don't!" The word was surprisingly hard to get out, and it was barely a whisper.

Rafe heard it, however, and his gaze swooped down to meet her own with swift concern.

"Don't be angry with me anymore," she murmured faintly, nestling her ear closer to the strong beat of his heart. "I'm so tired."

Rafe's arms tightened fiercely about her. "Why are you so damn stupid?" he asked huskily, pressing a soft kiss on her temple. "Why the hell did you run away? I've been going crazy. I must have searched ten miles of that beach tonight."

"Sorry," she murmured drowsily. The shadowy planes of his face were harsh above her, and lines of pain were graven about his lips. She reached up to trace those lines, but it suddenly seemed too much of an effort, and her hand fell limply back to her side. "I didn't mean to cause you any trouble."

"Shut up, damn it," Rafe said raggedly, his stride escalating as he neared the house. "For God's sake, just be quiet, Janna."

She obediently subsided and closed her eyes, cuddling closer to his warm strength with the confiding trust of a small child. She must have dozed, for the next moment of awareness was of being placed gently on the black velvet coverlet on the king-sized bed in the master suite.

Rafe's hands were quickly stripping her, pulling the damp pink velvet dress over her head and tossing it carelessly aside.

"No," she murmured protestingly, opening drowsy eyes. "Don't do that. I'm cold, Rafe."

His hands were busy removing her bra and bikini panties. "You're more than that," he said grimly. "You're half frozen." He looked down at her bare feet and drew a long, shaky breath. "Where the hell are your shoes?"

"I don't know. I must have lost them somewhere," she said vaguely.

Rafe growled another impatient imprecation and was stripping off his clothes while she watched him dreamily. Was he going to make love to her? She was a little tired, but she had no doubt Rafe would make her forget about that. He had only to touch her and she was on fire. She could use a little of that fire now. She was so cold.

Then she was being carried again, this time into the bathroom. Rafe let her slide down his body to the floor while he opened the door of the shower stall and adjusted the spray, still holding her cradled against his warmth. When the temperature of the water met with his approval, he drew her underneath the water and closed the shower door, still holding her in that deliciously protective embrace.

The hot water poured over them in a wonderfully warming stream, while Rafe's hands gently massaged her back and shoulders. Her arms slipped around his waist, her hands linked loosely as she stood lost in dreamy contentment while the steamy heat seemed to seep into her very bones. Rafe's hands left her back and reached behind her to the overhead rack. Then they were buried in her hair, gently massaging the shampoo into her salt-laden tresses. It was marvelously soothing, and she murmured in contentment, her arms tightening around Rafe's waist. She felt a butterfly kiss on her brow, and then he was rinsing her hair under the spray, his hands carefully guarding her face and eyes from the shampoo. It gave her a warmly treasured feeling to be so gently cosseted, and she opened her eyes to tell him so.

His face was frowningly intent. "Shut your eyes," he said gruffly. "You'll get soap in them."

A smile of tender amusement curved her lips as she closed her eyes once more and stood docilely while he painstakingly rinsed the shampoo out of her hair. She had heard that rough note of growling concern before. Only then, it had been uttered by a lioness chastising her mischievous cub.

"I'm glad you're so happy," Rafe said dryly as he turned off the water and opened the shower door. "I should have known putting me through hell would amuse you." He enfolded her in an enormous bath towel and was drying her with incredible gentleness, despite the roughness of his tone.

"You seem to be making a habit of this," she said bemusedly. He threw away the first towel and swaddled her securely in a big bath sheet before lifting her onto the vanity.

"It wouldn't be necessary if you wouldn't be so blasted careless about yourself," he said twisting a towel, turban fashion, about her head. "Don't you know people can die of exposure in temperatures warmer than this?" He was drying himself now, with brisk efficiency, and he paused to stare at her accusingly.

Janna's lips quirked involuntarily. What diverse elements composed the character of this man? For a moment he'd looked like a cross little boy, yet at other times he was the most aggressively mature male she'd ever known.

He threw his towel down on the vanity and scooped her up again. She was beginning to feel like a bundle of laundry, she thought humorously as Rafe tucked her into bed and climbed in beside her, pulling the velvet cover over both of them.

"I can't move," she complained, trying to extricate her arms from the towel swathing her like a straitjacket.

"Lie still," he ordered curtly, pulling her blanketed

form into his arms and burying his face in the hollow of her throat.

"But I feel like a mummy," she protested, wriggling to escape the suffocating folds of terry cloth. "Rafe, I can't breathe. At least let me—" She broke off abruptly. It wasn't possible, was it? Yet the tiny drop of moisture on her throat was real, and Rafe's lashes pressed against her flesh were undeniably damp. "Rafe?" she asked uncertainly.

"I thought you were dead," he said, his voice muffled against her. "I thought you'd fallen from that cliff onto the rocks below and been washed out to sea. I almost went crazy when I couldn't find you. Damn it! Damn it all to hell! You had no right to do that to me!"

"I didn't mean to worry you," she said hesitantly, lying very still in his arms. "I guess I didn't think. I just didn't want to go back to the house."

"Do you think I don't know that?" he growled, and she caught her breath at the aching torment in his voice. "I knew I'd hurt and humiliated you before I left you in the garden tonight. I guess I wanted to get a little of my own back." His arms tightened around her. "But you didn't have to run away. You knew that I wouldn't touch Marina."

She smiled tenderly at the accusing note in his voice. "I don't see how I could," she said softly. "You seemed pretty determined."

He ignored that with sublime arrogance. "You should have known I wouldn't want anyone but you," he insisted stubbornly. "You had no right to scare me like that."

"I won't do it again," she assured him solemnly, a thread of laughter running through her voice.

"It's not funny, damn it," he said, raising his head to look down at her with a frown. Then, as he met her eyes, his granite-hard features softened, his dark eyes becoming liquidly gentle and the curve of his mouth beautifully tender. "I want to tell you

THE LADY AND THE UNICORN • 155

something," he said huskily. "When I was running all over that blasted beach, not knowing if I'd ever see you again, I made a discovery. You know that emotion that neither of us knows anything about? I found I've become a world-class expert on the subject."

Janna felt her heart leap in her breast as if it had been touched by an electric current, and her eyes widened in shock. "Rafe," she breathed softly.

He put his hand swiftly on her lips. "No, don't say anything," he said quietly. "I know you don't feel the same way. I just made myself a promise that if I found you still alive I'd tell you how I felt." He settled her back in his arms, her turbaned head resting in the curve of his shoulder. "Now, go to sleep," he ordered softly. "You've had quite a night, Pocahontas."

Just like that he expected her to close her eyes and drift off into the arms of Morpheus, Janna thought wonderingly. Just as if he hadn't given her this incredibly selfless gift in those few simple sentences. He had sacrificed his ego and pride with a generosity that caused her throat to ache with tears. She was suddenly fiercely proud and ambivalently humble, and she was experiencing such a glowing burst of emotion it made her dizzy.

Then she was struggling out of the cocoon of toweling he'd wrapped about her. As she struggled out of the last folds, her arms went around him and she pressed the length of her body to the hardness of his. "I don't want to go to sleep," she said huskily. Her lips brushed lovingly against the hard bone of his shoulders. "Love me, Rafe."

He stiffened against her, then slowly pushed her away from him a little to look down at her sternly. "Look, I didn't make that little confession to play on your sympathies," he said. "Nor do I intend to wrest any sexual favors from you, after what you've been through tonight."

Her hand traveled in a slow, caressing movement from the hollow of his back to the hard, tight curve of his buttocks. "Would it be okay if I wrest a few from you, then?" she asked mischievously, pinching him gently.

He drew a shuddering breath, and she could feel his body hardening against her in arousal. His arms tightened slowly about her even as he said huskily, "We shouldn't do this. I meant to let you rest tonight. I wanted to take care of you."

"You've taken very good care of me," she assured him softly, her tongue tasting the delicious warmth of the skin of his throat. "Now let me take care of you." One leg moved to capture him in the warm security of her thighs, and he gave a low groan that came from the center of his being. His hips jerked against her compulsively, as if searching blindly for their home.

"Janna," he gasped, his face taut with need.

"Love me, Rafe," she murmured again, this time more insistently. "Love me." Then she brought him into the sweet warmth that was the end of his quest.

Janna could tell even in the wildest moments of their passion that Rafe was trying to restrain himself, to give her the gentleness and tenderness he thought she needed. She wouldn't permit it. He had given her too much tonight already. It was her turn to be the benefactor. She'd been through so much tonight, she knew she wouldn't be able to sustain any physical effort for very long, but it must be long enough for her to give Rafe this gift of pleasure. To do it, though, she must overcome Rafe's scruples about assuring himself of her satisfaction. She set about deliberately teasing him, until he lost control and began to plunge with mindless urgency, intent only on satisfying the hunger she'd aroused in him. When he collapsed against her with a deep groan that caused a shudder to wrack his entire body, she felt a deep, glowing satisfaction she'd never known before. Her arms clutched him fiercely to her, not wanting to let him go.

Rafe raised himself to look down at her uncertainly. "Janna, you didn't . . . ?"

She shook her head, her brown eyes glowing with tenderness. "It doesn't matter," she said softly. "Later, perhaps. I just want to hold you now."

He lay down beside her, cuddling her close. She could feel that precious dampness of his lashes against her temple. "God, I wish you hadn't done that," he said huskily. "I was psyching myself up to letting you go. I just might have made it." His lips brushed gently against her cheekbone. "It's too late now, Janna. I couldn't let you go now if I tried. It would destroy me."

Janna was almost asleep. The rigors of the evening combined with the warm contentment of this lovely moment had acted as a soporific. She heard Rafe's words only dimly, but there was something she knew she must say to him. She frowned in drowsy puzzlement, trying to pierce the misty cloud closing in on her. Then she realized she hadn't told Rafe that she loved him. That she never wanted to leave him no matter what price she'd have to pay.

"Rafe . . ."

"Shhh," he interrupted softly. "Go to sleep, baby. You're exhausted."

He was right, she thought sleepily. She couldn't keep her eyes open another moment. They could always talk in the morning. She would tell him tomorrow that she loved him.

Nine

But Rafe was gone when next Janna opened her eyes. She knew why when she glanced at the clock on the bedside table. It was almost one o'clock. She shook her head ruefully as she threw back the covers and jumped out of bed. During the night her improvised turban had slipped off, and her hair was a wild aureole about her face.

She grimaced as she looked into the mirror, picked up the brush and applied herself vigorously to brushing the wild mop until it shimmered with highlights, then braided it in her customary style. Twenty minutes later she had showered, dressed in white stovepipe jeans and a peach cowl-neck sweater and was running lightly down the stairs in search of Rafe.

Pat Dawson was crossing the foyer, heading in the direction of the library, and he glanced up with an appreciative grin. "Very nice," he drawled, his eyes twinkling. "But then, you should look absolutely glowing after lolling in bed half the day. It's we peasants who toil from sunrise to sunset who have that lean, haggard look."

"Yes, the lot of executive assistants is a woeful one," Janna agreed lightly. "Is Rafe around?"

Dawson gestured to the closed library door with the manilla folder he held in his hand. "He's on the phone to Tokyo at the moment. There's been some labor dispute in the electronics plant there. Shall I ask him if he can see you?"

Janna shrugged. "It's not important," she said cheerfully. "I'll talk to him later. I think I'll go up to the gazebo for an hour or two. I'll see if I can't persuade Stokley to purloin some bread and cheese from the chef." She made a face. "The last time I asked him for a picnic lunch he sent me out a meal that could have fed an army."

"He probably considers your spartan instincts an insult to his expertise," Pat said with a grin. "You've rather set Santine's household in a turmoil, Janna." His lips quirked ruefully. "Which reminds me, you're not planning on disappearing, as you did yesterday afternoon, are you? I don't think I'm up to facing another one of Mr. Santine's furies quite so soon."

"I'll be back long before he even knows I'm gone," she promised lightly. "Particularly if he's as busy as you say he is."

"I'd appreciate that," Pat said dryly, and he turned back toward the library. "This blasted strike is going to annoy him quite enough, without anything else's stirring him up."

"Has the countess left for San Francisco yet?" Janna asked idly as she watched him stride briskly across the foyer.

Dawson nodded. "Early this morning," he replied over his shoulder. "And not at all pleased, from the look of her."

Janna grinned happily. "How unfortunate," she murmured. As Pat disappeared into the library, she almost skipped across the foyer toward the kitchen.

Thirty minutes later she was sitting in the gazebo munching on deliciously crisp French bread and provolone and gazing out over the seascape with a feeling of infinite well-being. It was difficult to believe that anything could go wrong in a world so beautiful. The sun on her face was warm and gentle, the breeze a soft caress, and her spirit as buoyant as the surf below her.

Why did everything seem so simple now? For weeks

she'd been perfectly miserable, torn between her growing love for Rafe and a fear that that love would chain her to a life as rigidly controlled as the one her grandmother had known. She'd fought against that velvet cage with a desperation that now seemed exaggerated and unimportant.

A granite-hard man had let one tear fall and muttered a few awkward, almost inarticulate words, and it had melted all opposition in the twinkling of an eye. Why had she been afraid? She was strong enough to face any challenge Rafe could offer her. Why shouldn't she take this gift that fate had given her? What had happened between them was so powerful, it had swept them from their separate chosen paths into this passionate union. There must be a reason and a purpose behind it, as there was for all the forces of nature, and she must accept it with her usual serenity.

She slowly finished her lunch and then reluctantly rose to her feet. She was tempted to stay a little longer, particularly as there was no telling how long Rafe would be tied up with Tokyo. But she'd promised Pat, and if by chance Rafe was free, he might want to see her as much as she did him. When she entered the house, it was to be met by Fred Stokley, a worried frown on his usually impassive face. Her sense of contentment vanished immediately, to be replaced by icy foreboding.

"There you are, Miss Cannon," he said, relief obvious in his voice. "I was just coming to get you. Mr. Dawson said you were at the gazebo when I inquired. You had an urgent phone call from a Mr. Jody Forrester. He asked that you return his call immediately, but when I was trying to locate you and told Mr. Santine, he said you were to come to the library at once."

Jody. Janna felt a chill sweep over her and an accompanying sensation of fear tighten the muscles of her stomach. "Oh, no," she breathed faintly. "Not now." There could only be one reason for an urgent call from Jody. That sense of something wrong in Jody's manner yesterday, and now this. "I'll call him right away," she murmured, brushing by Stokley hurriedly on the way to the phone in the foyer.

He followed her. "But Mr. Santine was quite insistent that you see him first before you returned Mr. Forrester's call," he protested, frowning, as she rapidly pushed the buttons on the phone.

"I can't speak to him now," she said impatiently, listening to the phone ringing on the other end in an agony of suspense. Why didn't he answer, damn it? "I'll see him later."

Stokley started to say something else, then shrugged and silently withdrew. Janna didn't even realize he'd left, for the phone was suddenly picked up.

"Jody?" Her voice was husky, and she could barely get the word out.

"It's over, Janna," Jody said gently.

Janna sagged against the mahogany table and closed her eyes as desolation swept over her. She had known the message Jody would give her, but she'd maintained that tiny fugitive hope. "When?"

"Yesterday afternoon, almost immediately after you called," he said quietly. "She'd been failing for the past week. She didn't want you to know."

"Yesterday," Janna said numbly. "Why didn't you call me then, Jody?"

"It was your grandmother's last request," Jody said, his voice husky. "She didn't want you to know until it was all over. She was cremated last night. She said you'd know what to do with the remains."

The hill. "Yes, I know," Janna said softly. "I'll take the first flight out, Jody. Will you meet me at the airport?"

"Of course," he said gruffly, clearing his throat. "Call me when you know what flight you'll be on."

"Thank you, Jody," she said gently. "Thank you for everything. I know this hasn't been easy for you."

"She was a great lady, Janna," Jody said gravely. "It was a privilege to know her. She's the one who deserves the gratitude. There aren't many people in the world who can expand your horizons just by simply being themselves. She gave me more than I gave her."

"She gave us all more," Janna said, blinking back the tears. "I'll see you in Sweetwater, Jody."

She replaced the receiver and slowly moved toward the staircase. From the corner of her eye she saw Stokley hovering worriedly in the arch of the lounge, but he didn't speak until she was halfway up the stairs. "Is everything all right, Miss Cannon?" he asked hesitantly. "Is there anything that I can do?"

"I'll need someone to drive me to the airport," Janna said quietly. "I'm leaving for Oklahoma at once. Will you take care of that for me, Stokley?"

"Of course, Miss Cannon," he said. "I'll attend to it right away. May I send someone up to help you with your packing?"

Janna shook her head. "I'll only be taking a few things," she answered. "I can take care of it myself. I'll be down within fifteen minutes."

"I'll have the car waiting for you, Miss Cannon," Stokley said briskly.

It took only a short time to pack her overnight case and call to make plane reservations. Janna snatched up a rust tweed jacket and hurried out of the bedroom, checking her watch as she did so. She had only a few minutes to speak to Rafe if she was to get to the airport in time to catch the commuter plane to Los Angeles.

She needn't have worried, for Rafe was standing waiting at the foot of the staircase, and she breathed a sigh of relief. "I was afraid you'd still be on the line to Tokyo," she said. "I have to talk to you, Rafe."

"I'm glad you were going to spare me a minute to say goodbye," Rafe said caustically, gripping her elbow and propelling her toward the library.

She'd been in such a bemused state that she hadn't noticed the fury darkening his face and the almost visible electric tension that was surrounding him. "Of course I was going to speak to you," Janna answered, frowning in bewilderment. "I wouldn't have just left without saying anything. That wouldn't be courteous."

He slammed the door behind them and whirled her around to face him, his expression strained. "And you wouldn't want to be guilty of a social *faux pas*, would you?" he asked with biting irony. "It wouldn't be polite to go to a new lover without saying a fond farewell to the old." Her stunned expression seemed to add fuel to his rage, for he gave her a hard shake. "Though your old college sweetheart can't be classified precisely as a new acquisition, can he?"

"Jody?" Janna asked, her eyes wide with shock and pain. She'd forgotten completely about Rafe's jealous display over Jody. Everything that had happened since had driven it completely from her mind. "You don't understand, Rafe. I'm not going home to renew a love affair, I have—"

"You're damn right you're not," Rafe said between his teeth. "You're not going anywhere. I won't have you running back to this Forrester without giving me a chance to persuade you to stay. I know it was my fault you were upset last night, but you can't just walk out on me. I won't have it!"

"I don't have time to argue with you. I have a plane to catch," Janna said tersely. She felt a flicker of anger start to simmer beneath the shock and sorrow she was feeling. Hadn't she enough to tolerate without this crazy jealousy of Rafe's raising its Medusa head? "It's clear that you're not going to listen to what I have to say, so I'll stop wasting my efforts." She shrugged off his hold and put her hand on the doorknob. "I'll call you when I get to the farm. Perhaps you'll be more in the mood to listen then."

She opened the door. His voice was darkly menacing behind her. "If you let him touch you, so help me God, I'll ruin him, Janna. You might remember that during your joyous reunion."

She cast him a glance over her shoulder that was brilliant with unshed tears. "Joyous?" she asked huskily. "I'm not expecting this homecoming to be very joyous. My grandmother died yesterday, Rafe."

Shock, then remorse, rapidly superseded the anger on Rafe's face, and his eyes narrowed in concern. He took an impulsive step forward. "Janna . . ."

But she was gone. He hesitated a moment, his face troubled, and then strode swiftly after her. He reached the front entrance too late to do anything but watch the black Lincoln wind its way down the driveway toward the gatehouse.

As he had promised, Jody met her at the small airport in Sweetwater, and she went into his arms like an animal in pain seeking refuge. He held her for a long, silent moment, his hands rubbing her back soothingly, as if she were a nervous mare. Then he pushed her quietly away, looking down into her face with a frown of concern on his blunt, plain face.

"Okay?" he asked gently, his hazel eyes worriedly raking over her strained features.

She nodded, blinking back the tears. "I'm fine. I'm just so glad you're here, Jody." It seemed, with the passing of her grandmother, that the last roots of her childhood had been pulled up and thrown to the winds of change. But here was Jody, with his tousled sandy hair with its familiar cowlick that would never stay down, and the tall, wiry body that was skeletally thin and persisted in remaining so no matter how much he ate. Even his faded jeans, dusty boots, and neat plaid shirt looked blessedly familiar.

"The pickup is in the parking lot," he said gruffly,

giving her another hug before releasing her. "Do you have any luggage to claim?"

Janna shook her head and indicated the overnight bag in her hand. "I figured that a carry-on bag would make things simpler." She smiled shakily. "I can always borrow a pair of jeans from you if I need to."

He nodded as he turned her gently in the direction of the door to the parking lot. "You're welcome to them if you don't raise your nose in scorn at plain ones these days," he said as he eyed the white stovepipe designer jeans she was wearing. "You've become very elegant for a country girl, Janna."

"Plain old jeans will be fine," she said quietly, not answering the obvious question in his expression. She had no desire to think about Rafe and the luxurious life she'd lived with him. Their parting was still too painfully fresh. His misunderstanding and lack of trust were still too hurtful for her to consider objectively. She was here for a purpose, and until that purpose was fulfilled, she must put aside any thought, any emotion that might distract from it. "Tell me about the past months, Jody. I want to know everything."

On the seventy-mile drive to the farm, Jody tried to do just that, answering her questions patiently and describing her grandmother's last days with a simple clarity that made every word and action vividly real to Janna. When the pickup finally pulled up before the familiar brick farmhouse, it was almost dusk, and there were no more words to be said.

"You've painted the shutters," Janna observed as Jody helped her out of the pickup and she slowly climbed the porch steps.

Jody nodded. "This spring. I figured I'd get around to the barn this fall." He opened the screen and then the green-and-white storm door, and stood aside for her to enter. "The farm will be yours now, Janna," he said hesitantly. "Have you thought about what you're going to do with it?"

She shook her head. "I guess I always assumed that you'd just take over, Jody. You've always wanted a farm of your own, and this is more your home than mine. We'll work something out." She looked over her shoulder at the hill rising in the distance, which was blazing with the myriad colors of autumn. "Except for our hill. I want to retain title to that."

"Of course," Jody said softly. He turned on the lights, illuminating the shabby comfort of the living room. "There's some soup on the stove. Could you eat a little?"

"Later, perhaps," she said, looking around at the familiar surroundings. The room looked smaller than she remembered, but everything else was the same. "I suppose I'd better go through Grandmother's things."

Jody shook his head. "There's nothing to do," he said quietly. "She started getting rid of things when she first learned she was ill. She didn't want you to have to do it later. By the time she was too ill to get out of bed there were only a few mementos left. She ordered me to burn them. There's nothing here now that would bring back memories."

"She thought of everything," Janna said huskily, her eyes brimming with tears. "She knew I wouldn't need any *thing* to remind me." She suddenly whirled and cried desperately, "Damn it, Jody, why can't we live forever? She shouldn't have had to die."

Jody shrugged helplessly. "The eternal question," he said, rubbing the back of his neck wearily. "I can't answer you, Janna." His eyes were warm and sympathetic. "She did leave you one final duty. The man from the funeral home is delivering her ashes to you tomorrow morning."

She drew a long, shaky breath. "I'll be ready," she said quietly. "I think I'd like to sleep in Grandmother's room tonight, if that would be all right."

"It's your house," Jody said with a shrug. "I have to go feed the stock. Would you like to come with me?"

She shook her head. "I'm tired and I think I'll get settled in," she said as she slipped out of her jacket. "And there's a phone call I have to make."

"Right," Jody said, turning toward the door. "I'll be back soon."

After he'd gone, Janna walked slowly into the bedroom. It was just as Jody had said—there was nothing in the pristine shabbiness of the little room to bring back memories. It had the impersonal coldness of a hotel room. She put her overnight case on the white chenille spread of the four-poster bed, placing her tweed jacket on top of it, before returning to the living room to pick up the telephone on the end table by the couch.

She dialed the Carmel number with mixed emotions. Though she was still resentful of Rafe's behavior, she felt a great desire to put things right between them. She needed the security of talking to Rafe and knowing that she had his understanding and support.

The remote precision of the voice on the other end of the line was undisputedly Stokley, though it did warm a trifle when she identified herself. There was even a trace of regret in his tone when he told her she would not be able to speak to either Mr. Santine or Mr. Dawson, as they'd both left for San Francisco almost immediately after her own departure.

"May I take a message in case Mr. Santine calls to inquire?" he asked courteously.

"No. There's no message," she said, trying to hide her disappointment and shock. "Thank you, Stokley." She replaced the receiver and stood there for a moment, feeling very much alone. She knew quite well Rafe had had no intention of leaving for San Francisco today. The only conclusion she could draw from his abrupt departure was that he was even more upset than she had believed. He hadn't even waited to see if she would keep her promise to call, before he'd left Carmel.

She drew a deep breath and squared her shoulders determinedly. The situation was no worse now than it had been before she made that call. She would just have to forget her own personal problems, as she had originally intended. She couldn't let doubts about the future spoil this last goodbye to the past.

She turned and strode swiftly out the front door and down the porch steps in search of Jody.

Ten

The empty silver cannister arched against the brilliance of the blue autumn sky; it appeared to linger for an instant at the apex of its flight before descending with cometlike speed to disappear into the depths of the lake.

It was done. Janna took a deep breath, and unconsciously drew her blue shirt closer about her, as if seeking warmth to ward off the chill of this last act, which completed the ritual. Then she turned swiftly and started to climb the hill, pacing herself so as to require a maximum of effort and prevent her from thinking. By the time she reached the top of the hill and settled in her favorite place, on the flat boulder overlooking the small lake in the valley below, she was breathless, her breasts heaving and the tears on her face almost dried by the warm breeze.

She didn't know how many hours she stayed there, gazing blindly at that spectacular autumn panorama before her. Beech gold, maple scarlet, and evergreen pine were woven in an earth tapestry against the cerulean background of the sky that was achingly beautiful. At first she was aware of none of it, but gradually she became conscious of the rustle of the breeze through the crisp autumn leaves. The whisper was oddly soothing, like a mother hushing her baby's tears. The warmth of the sun on her upraised face and throat was like a gentle caress, and the aromatic scents of earth and grass surrounded her in an embrace that was comfortingly familiar.

She could feel the pain inside her loosen its painful knot, and she let it go. She knew an instant of quiet, joyous release, and then a peaceful serenity that seemed to fill every corner of her spirit. She closed her eyes and murmured the farewell that was not goodbye. Always. Always with her. Those were the words her grandmother had spoken to Jody, and now that Janna had released the pain, she could accept them.

The sun was low, and the vivid hue of the sky was fading to a hazy gray-blue, when she heard the sound of firm footsteps crunching on the dry leaves behind her. It must be Jody checking to see if she was all right, she thought dreamily.

"I'm fine, Jody," she said quietly, not looking over her shoulder. "I was about to come down. There was no need for you to come after me."

The rustling of the leaves was right behind her now, and she suddenly felt a warm, heavy hand on her shoulder. "You're wrong, Janna," Rafe said softly. "I'll always need to come after you, wherever you are."

Janna tensed beneath his hand, as a fierce tide of joy surged through her. Then she slowly relaxed and looked up at the man standing beside her. "Always is a long time," she said quietly. "I've been thinking quite a bit about that today." Despite the first shock of surprise it seemed oddly right that Rafe be here now, at this time, in this place.

"I imagine you have," Rafe said gravely as he came around to stand before her. He should have looked ridiculously out of place, in these surroundings, in his faultless dark-blue business suit and crisp white shirt, she thought absently. Yet he appeared as comfortable here as he did in the library at Santine's Castle, and as casually uncaring of his sartorial elegance. He dropped to his knees in front of her

and gathered her hands in his. "I had a long talk
with your friend Jody before he would tell me where
you were and what you were doing." His dark eyes
were warm and intent as they met her own. "I've
been thinking a lot about that word, too, Janna. I
didn't use it lightly."

Her gaze clung to his for a brief moment, and she
felt the familiar breathless melting sensation before
her eyes slid away from his. "You look tired," she
said quietly, moistening her lips nervously. He looked
worse than that. There was nothing even in the
least boyish about Rafe today. He looked every one of
his thirty-eight years, with those mauve shadows
beneath the snapping vitality of his dark eyes, and
deeply graven lines around his lips.

"And you look very serene and composed," he said
wryly. "Quite a juxtaposition. I came rushing halfway across the country to comfort you, and find you
don't need me at all. It's most deflating, Pocahontas."

Her eyes flew back to his face, and her hands
tightened instinctively on his own. "I need you," she
said softly. "I tried to call you last night, but you'd
left for San Francisco. I thought you were still angry
with me."

He shook his head. "I left in such a hurry I forgot
to tell Stokley to get in touch with me if you rang."
He frowned. "Why in the hell didn't you leave a
number? When I remembered you said you might call,
I phoned the Castle, but it was too late. The number
here is unlisted, and it took Dawson half the evening to pry it out of the telephone company. By that
time we were so damn busy I didn't get time to call."

"Trouble with your Tokyo negotiations?" Janna
asked, experiencing a twinge of disappointment.

"Trouble with negotiations, all right, but not with
Tokyo," Rafe said obscurely. "These were much more
delicate in nature."

"Another take-over?" Janna asked lightly. "Will I
be reading about it in the paper next week?"

"I hope it's going to be a very amicable merger," Rafe replied, his dark eyes twinkling. "And I assure you that you won't have to read about it in the paper." His gaze dropped to her hands, clasped in his, and his thumbs idly began a gentle massage at the pulse points of her wrist. "You know how sorry I am about your grandmother," he said soberly. "I felt like a complete bastard when you dropped that little bomb on me before you left the Castle." His lips twisted bitterly. "The one time in your life when you needed someone, I had to blow it. I was so filled with my own petty insecurities and jealousies that I couldn't see beyond the fact that you were leaving me. It seemed as if I'd been waiting and dreading your walking out of my life since the moment I met you. I should have been prepared for it, but I went a little crazy, I guess."

"If you'd only listened to me, I'd have told you everything, Rafe," Janna said gently. "I've tried to talk to you so many times in the past weeks, but I just couldn't get past the wall you'd built around yourself."

He didn't look up. "I was afraid," he said gruffly. Then, at her shocked exclamation, his hands tightened on hers. "I felt as if I were bleeding inside. You made it pretty damn clear that you didn't feel the same torment I was going through, and I resented it. Not only was I head over heels in love, but it had to be with a woman who didn't give a damn for me." He laughed mirthlessly. "I wanted to possess and know every facet of you—your mind, your emotions, your memories. The only thing you'd let me have was your body, and for the first time in my life that wasn't enough for me." He looked up, and Janna felt a queer catch at her heart at the pain in his eyes. "My ego demanded that you love me as much as I loved you," he said huskily. "I thought I couldn't tolerate being the eternal supplicant at your door."

"Rafe." His name was wonderfully tender on her

lips. She wanted to bring him close to her, to hold him in her arms, and banish all the pain and uncertainty he'd known. "Rafe, it won't—"

He put his hand gently on her lips, stopping her. "You don't have to say anything," he said softly. "I'm not trying to lay any guilt trips on you. I don't care any more if I'm the lover and not the loved. The only thing that's important to me now is keeping you in my life. I can take anything as long as I know that you're by my side." He frowned thoughtfully. "I think I've got it worked out. Will you listen to my proposition?"

"It seems I have no choice," Janna replied resignedly, her lips quirking. "I certainly can't get you to listen to me."

"Later," he said absently, lifting her hand to kiss her palm lingeringly. "I've been thinking about this all night, and I've got to get it out on the table."

"By all means," she said solemnly, her brown eyes twinkling. "I'd be foolish to obstruct the path of a great tycoon in action. Better individuals than I have ended up flatter than a pancake beneath your wheels."

"I did it again, didn't I?" Rafe asked ruefully, pulling a face. "I meant to be very reasonable and considerate, even humble. I'm afraid it's not the nature of the beast."

Humble? Rafe Santine? Janna smothered a smile. "I've noticed that," she said. "I find it very praiseworthy of you to even make the attempt."

He frowned suspiciously. "Are you laughing at me?" he growled. Then, dismissing it as unimportant, he continued with his usual single-mindedness. "Oh, well, I'll be humble and considerate later," he said crisply. "Right now, just listen to me, damn it."

"Yes, sir," Janna said with equal briskness. "I'm listening, sir."

He gave her a quelling glance. "You're not helping matters," he accused. "I'm trying to make you an offer." Without waiting for her to reply, he went on. "The way I see it, you have no really valid objection to staying with me. We're very compatible in the normal course of events. I can provide you with everything you could possibly want materially. In addition, you can't deny that sexually we're dynamite together."

"No, I can't deny that," she agreed, her lips twitching.

"The only drawback I can see you might find to any long-term relationship is that you might feel I would inhibit your freedom, either personally or career-wise." His eyes narrowed on her face. "Am I correct in believing that's your primary concern?"

"It's certainly something to think about," she said lightly. She always enjoyed watching Rafe the businessman in action, and it was a novel experience to have his acumen turned in her direction.

"Then, I think I can put your fears to rest on that score," he said coolly. "I think you'll agree that once given, my word can be trusted?"

"Oh, indubitably," Janna said gravely. It was strange to remember how vital she would have considered this discussion only a few days ago. Now she was having a problem even taking it seriously. The only thing that was truly important was the fact that Rafe loved her. Given that, she was serenely confident everything else could be worked out.

Rafe was looking distinctly displeased with her levity, so she tried to look appropriately earnest. "I'll give you my word that you'll have absolute liberty in all aspects of our life together," he said crisply. "You may come and go as you please, wherever your work takes you. I won't insist on marriage or any other commitment from you unless you find that you're pregnant." He glanced at her flat stomach. "I can't deny I regard that circumstance as something to be desired. It would solve a hell of a lot of problems for me. I will, however, promise that from now on it will be your choice whether you wish to carry my child."

"Very generous," she murmured ironically.

"More generous than you think," he said grimly. "I had no wish to give up that particular lever." He unclasped one of her hands, and she felt the warmth of his large hand on her belly through the denim fabric of her jeans. "I like the idea of my child growing in you."

She liked the idea, too, she thought, with an almost primitive thrill of acknowledgment. Just thinking about it had a physical effect on her body. She felt a hot, melting warmth in the center of her being, and the muscles of her stomach tightened beneath Rafe's gentle massaging hand, her breasts suddenly heavy and ripe with need beneath Jody's blue chambray work shirt.

It was impossible to hide her sudden arousal, particularly from Rafe, who was intimately familiar with her body and its responses. His eyes darkened to warm intensity as they met hers, and his hand continued the slow, gentle massage with even greater deliberateness. "You'd make a wonderful mother, Janna," he said huskily. "Strong, intelligent, loving. Our son would be so lucky in you." He released her other hand and slowly unbuttoned her shirt, while she watched him with eyes clouded with desire. When her breasts were bared, he lowered his head slowly, and his lips sucked deliciously at one engorged nipple. "You'll be so damn beautiful with your breasts heavy with milk, little earth mother," he said hoarsely. "I'm already jealous of my own child. I don't want to share anything about you." He gave the other nipple a lingering kiss, and reluctantly drew the material of the shirt closed. He shook his head as if to clear it, his eyes drawn compulsively to the hard buttons of her nipples, which were poking saucily at the material of the shirt. "Where was I?" he asked absently.

Janna gave him a glance of rueful exasperation.

His single-mindedness was no longer so amusing when her body was on fire for the satisfaction that only he could give her—and evidently had no intention of granting her at the moment. "I haven't the slightest idea," she said crossly.

"Oh, yes," Rafe pulled his eyes from those impudent nipples with some difficulty and lowered them determinedly to the leaf-carpeted ground. "As I was saying, it will be entirely your choice. While you're with me, naturally, you'll have unlimited capital at your disposal. You need only to ask, and anything that I can give you, either monetarily or in terms of clout, will be yours." He glanced up into her face. "I know it probably won't mean a damn to you, but you'd possess a staggering amount of power through me."

"Crowns and scepters never appealed to me," Janna said tartly, wishing he'd stop the sales pitch and just take her in his arms. She *wanted* him, damn it!

"I'm well aware of that," he said gloomily. "Why couldn't you have just a hint of avariciousness in your makeup? It would make my position a hell of a lot stronger." His face brightened, "There *is* one lever that I can use. Your precious endangered species. Can you imagine what a patron with my influence would do for your cause? Now, how can you refuse a gift like that?"

"It would be very difficult," she agreed tersely. "Are you quite finished now?"

He nodded warily, his eyes on her face. "I think that covers all the bases," he said slowly. "Have I convinced you what a fool you'd be to turn me down?"

"Have you ever failed in any take-over bid?" she asked him lightly. "I'm dazzled and intimidated by your logic and generosity."

"This isn't funny, Janna," he said tightly. "This is important to me. Are you going to stay with me?"

"It's not a decision to be made lightly," she said,

her lashes demurely hiding the teasing glint in her eyes. "But I must admit that you're a very persuasive man, Rafe. I can tell you really care for me. Your proposition was as impassioned as a proposal for a merger between IBM and Xerox."

"That wouldn't be as sterile a fusion as you're implying," Rafe said dryly. "And you can bet *our* merger would be very passionate, Janna."

"I think I'd require assurance up front on that score," she said softly.

His eyes widened in surprise. It seemed she had managed to disconcert him, she thought mischievously. "I don't think I understand," he said carefully.

"I think you do," Janna said, her brown eyes twinkling. "But perhaps I can help." She slowly stood up, leisurely unzipped her jeans, slid them down her hips, and stepped out of them.

"Here? Now?" Rafe asked, moistening his dry lips with the tip of his tongue as the minute silk bikini panties followed the jeans. She stepped casually out of her tan moccasins.

Her hands closed on the open lapels of the blue work shirt. "Right here. Right now," she said softly, looking down at him lovingly. "This is a very special place for me. I want to share it with you. I want to give you all my memories of the past and create a few new ones for the future. Will you do that for me, Rafe?"

She was kneeling facing him now, her eyes fixed steadily on his face. He made no move to touch her, his muscles tense and still. "Why, Janna? Why do you want to give me your memories?"

"For a brilliant businessman, you're regrettably lacking in perception, Rafe Santine," she said tenderly. "If you'd let me speak instead of using your usual bulldozer tactics, you'd know the answer. God knows I've been trying to tell you since the night before last."

"I'm listening now," he said tersely, his hands

closing urgently on her shoulders. "Tell me, damn it."

"I love you," she said simply.

"You love . . ." His voice trailed off. His face was suddenly lit with a joy and tenderness that Janna knew she'd remember for the rest of her life. Then that fleeting, beautifully vulnerable expression was gone, and he was frowning fiercely at her. "You should have made me listen," he said gruffly, giving her a little shake. "You mean I've been suffering the torment of the damned for an entire two days, when you could have put me out of my misery with just a simple sentence?"

"I've been a little occupied during that time, if you'll recall," she replied gently.

His face softened remorsefully, and he pulled her swiftly into his arms. "God, I'm sorry," he said huskily. "I can never seem to do anything right with you, love. I don't deserve you." He pressed a gentle kiss on her temple. "But I'm sure as hell going to take you." His arms tightened around her. "And speaking of taking, I believe that you voiced a request."

"I believe I did," she replied gravely, her brown eyes twinkling. "But you're taking your own sweet time about granting it. Perhaps I'd better reconsider your offer, despite your very generous terms."

"Too late," he said throatily, his hands swiftly working the chambray shirt down her arms to fall in a pool of blue in the leaves on which they were kneeling. "You promised to take me into your heart and your mind as well as your body, but I'll take what I can get at the moment." He pushed her away from him and shrugged out of his jacket, his fingers rapidly unbuttoning his white shirt.

As he spread his coat on the pile of leaves, a large business envelope fell out of his inner pocket. Janna picked it up and proffered it casually.

He shook his head with a mocking grin as he

slipped out of his shirt. "That belongs to you. I forgot to give it to you." Then, as she continued to look at him with puzzled eyes, he explained absently. "It was going to be my ace in the hole in case you turned me down, but now you can consider it a wedding present."

"I gather you're reneging on the noncommitment clause in your proposition," Janna said teasingly, admiring the smooth, brawny muscles of his shoulders. "Next you'll want me to give up my work and try to keep me barefoot and pregnant."

"The idea has appeal," he said lightly, throwing his belt aside and unzipping his pants. "I'd probably go for it, if I thought I could get away with it." His smile faded, and his face became grave. "You needn't worry about that, Janna. I want you to be so happy you'll never want to leave me. I'll keep my promises to you on all the other points. Is it too much to ask you to give me this?"

She shook her head. "No, it's not too much," she said softly, feeling a surge of love for him so strong it seemed to fill every atom of her being. "I want to be committed to you, Rafe Santine. I don't think a lifetime is going to be long enough for me to belong to you."

"Belong?" he asked quietly. "That's a strange term for someone who values her freedom as much as you, Janna."

"It's one of the things that I've been thinking about while I've been sitting here." Janna said tranquilly, sitting back on her heels dreamily to appraise his now-naked body. "It's very simple, really. You can't possess without being possessed. It's possible to build your own prison with bars of loneliness and fear." She smiled gently. "I'll have my freedom, Rafe, and I'll savor it and hold it the more dearly for the night, when I return to your arms."

They were both silent for a long moment, kneeling as naked and unashamed as Adam and Eve on that hillside, and the look that they exchanged was as grave and meaningful as a solemn vow.

Rafe cleared his throat, but his voice was still husky as he said, "You haven't looked at your present yet."

She reluctantly tore her eyes away from that look, which seemed to be supplying her with answers to questions she hadn't even known existed, and glanced down at the envelope in her hand. "Can't it wait until later?" she asked. She wanted to be close to him. She wanted him in her arms and in her body.

"No, you lustful wench," Rafe said firmly. "I spent a sleepless night and several exasperating, frustrating phone calls to arrange that particular gift, and the least you can do is to look at it and thank me for it." He cast a rueful glance down at his own obvious arousal. "Quickly. Very quickly, please."

Janna grinned mischievously as she opened the envelope. Her brow creased in puzzlement as she noticed that its only contents were two black-and-white photographs. She drew them out slowly and stared in blank surprise.

"The one standing upright is Norbet; he's the male from the zoo in Ceylon," Rafe said. "The one by the rock pool is Celene, a female from the London Zoo." He frowned. "Or perhaps it's the other way around." He made a wry face. "It's no wonder pandas are having problems reproducing. You can't tell the damn things apart."

"I believe it's safe to assume that they can tell the difference," she said absently, still looking down at the pictures.

"I wouldn't be too sure," Rafe said skeptically. "You might explore that possibility when they're delivered to the Camino Reserve next month. It might be the answer to the whole question of the endangered species."

Janna's eyes widened in surprise. "Delivered?" she said faintly. "You *bought* those two panda bears?"

He nodded. "And at no little cost to my temper," he said grimly. "Do you know how difficult it is to get hold of a male and female panda? I've never experienced such suspicion in my entire life. I think they thought I wanted their heads to hang over my mantel."

There was such disgust in his tone that Janna had to laugh despite the tears that were brimming in her eyes. What a beautifully touching gesture for Rafe to have made.

"Do you like your wedding present, Pocahontas?" Rafe asked softly, watching her face with a tenderness that caused her breath to catch in her throat and her heart to flutter strangely.

"I love my wedding present," she assured him huskily. "I'm sure it's unique in the annals of marital history."

"Great," Rafe said as he gently pulled her into his arms, the hard warmth of his flesh branding her own from breast to thigh. "God, you feel good," he muttered hoarsely. His hands moved in tender exploration over the slender curve of her back and buttocks. "So soft, yet so firm and womanly." One hand moved around to cup her full breast in his palm. "Very womanly. There's no doubt which one is the female in this species. Much more convenient."

There was no question regarding Rafe's masculinity either, Janna thought happily as her arms slid around his shoulders, her fingers curling in the crispness of the hair at his nape. "Yes, far more convenient," she murmured lovingly, and he bore her back on the coat he had spread on the rustling leaves.

The moment was inexpressibly beautiful, Janna thought dreamily as Rafe bent over her, his dark face intent and his lips curved in an expression of passionate tenderness. She could see the canopy of blue sky over Rafe's shoulders and the brilliance of the autumn leaves on the oak tree above her. Completion and renewal. The cycle went on forever, not only in nature, but in the heart. How thrilling to know that.

"Hey," Rafe said gently, gazing down at her glowing brown eyes and absorbed expression. "Come back to me, Janna. I need you with me."

She smiled at him with such loving warmth that he caught his breath.

"I'm with you, Rafe," she said softly. "Always."

Then she pulled him down to begin once again her own ritual of completion and renewal.

THE EDITOR'S CORNER

Our LOVESWEPT romance publishing program increases from three to four titles every month with our February list. We hope you'll feel that each of our love stories next month is a special Valentine's Day present—long-stemmed, exquisite yellow roses from Iris Johansen; a delectable selection of bon-bons from Kay Hooper; a warmly satisfying vintage wine from Dorothy Garlock; a bottle of haunting and evocative perfume from Fayrene Preston.

THE GOLDEN VALKYRIE, #31, is another dramatic and fast-paced love story from Iris Johansen whose works you've written such glowing letters about since we introduced her last August. In this gripping, yet often highly amusing tale, the "golden valkyrie" is the large, but very lovely private detective Honey Winston. The hero is a much publicized member of royalty known as "Lusty Lance." And the episode that brings these two characters together is as surprising as it is delightful. But Honey quickly sees the real man and the sensitive artist behind the gossip column image of the outrageously attractive Prince Rubinoff. And, armed with insights and a tender commitment to him, she sets out to free him from his gilded, but limited existence. This is a passionate and truly exciting story.

C.J.'S FATE, #32, is witty and wonderful . . . another of those delicious confections we've come to expect Kay Hooper to whip up for us. We at Bantam are delighted to welcome Kay as a LOVESWEPT author and to present this romance as her first—but certainly not her only—LOVESWEPT. We think you'll

(continued)

laugh out loud throughout this charming story of an unsuspecting woman who discovers romance when and where she least expects it; you'll sigh a lot, too, over the winsome tenderness of Kay's dashing hero—and his efforts to woo his lovely lady. Right along with C.J. you'll keep falling harder and harder for the wise, funny, and deeply romantic lawyer who plays havoc with her emotions!

THE PLANTING SEASON #33, is another of the heartwarming, believable romances for which Dorothy Garlock is known and loved by a legion of devoted fans. Set on a working farm, **THE PLANTING SEASON** is uniquely American, a harvest of touching emotion for the reader. Dorothy's heroine, Iris Ouverson, is a mature woman, experienced in dealing with the vagaries of the elements, yet innocent about romance. Against her will, Iris is forced to share the land she loves with a stranger, John Lang, who knows nothing of the hardships of wrenching a living from the earth, yet seems to know too much about how to sweep a woman off her feet. As touching as Dorothy's first LOVESWEPT (#6, **A LOVE FOR ALL TIME**), **THE PLANTING SEASON** is a romance you won't want to miss!

In LOVESWEPT #21, **THE SEDUCTION OF JASON,** published last October, Fayrene Preston introduced a secondary character—the kooky, absolutely unique, and very touching Samuelina Adkinson. "Sami," as she's known to her friends (and oh what a large and varied group that is!), now has her own romance: **FOR THE LOVE OF SAMI,** #34. Daniel Parker-St. James is the sort of hero around whom romantic fantasies must be woven—a man who is tender, considerate, passionate, powerful. And all the promise that Fayrene, demonstrated in her three previous works is fulfilled magnificently in this vibrant, extraordinary love story!

Roses ... Candy ... Rare wine ... Haunting perfume—the "gifts" of the four LOVESWEPTS for Valentine's Day. And they aren't fattening or intoxicating and they certainly aren't perishable! In fact, we hope you enjoy each LOVESWEPT so much that you will keep it to enjoy again and again as time goes by. With warm good wishes,

Carolyn Nichols

Carolyn Nichols
Editor
LOVESWEPT
Bantam Books, Inc.
666 Fifth Avenue
New York, NY 10103

Love Stories you'll never forget
by authors you'll always remember

Love Stories you'll never forget by authors you'll always remember

☐	21630	**LIGHTNING THAT LINGERS #25** Sharon & Tom Curtis	$1.95
☐	21631	**ONCE IN A BLUE MOON #26** Billie J. Green	$1.95
☐	21632	**THE BRONZED HAWK #27** Iris Johansen	$1.95
☐	21637	**LOVE, CATCH A WILD BIRD #28** Anne Reisser	$1.95
☐	21626	**THE LADY AND THE UNICORN #29** Iris Johansen	$1.95
☐	21628	**WINNER TAKE ALL #30** Nancy Holder	$1.95

Prices and availability subject to change without notice.

Buy them at your local bookstore or use this handy coupon for ordering:

Bantam Books, Inc., Dept. SW, 414 East Golf Road, Des Plaines, Ill. 60016

Please send me the books I have checked above. I am enclosing $_____
(please add $1.25 to cover postage and handling). Send check or money order
—no cash or C.O.D.'s please.

Mr/Mrs/Miss _____

Address_____

City_____ State/Zip_____

SW2—1/84

Please allow four to six weeks for delivery. This offer expires 7/84.

SPECIAL
MONEY SAVING
OFFER

Now you can have an up-to-date listing of Bantam's hundreds of titles plus take advantage of our unique and exciting bonus book offer. A special offer which gives you the opportunity to purchase a Bantam book for only 50¢. Here's how!

By ordering any five books at the regular price per order, you can also choose any other single book in the catalog (up to a $4.95 value) for just 50¢. Some restrictions do apply, but for further details why not send for Bantam's illustrated Shop-At-Home Catalog today!

Just send us your name and address plus 50¢ to defray the postage and handling costs.